HAUNT ME

HAUNT ME

K. R. Alexander

Scholastic Inc.

Copyright © 2020 by Alex R. Kahler writing as K. R. Alexander

All rights reserved. Published by Scholastic Inc., *Publishers since 1920.* SCHOLASTIC and associated logos are trademarks and/or registered trademarks of Scholastic Inc.

The publisher does not have any control over and does not assume any responsibility for author or third-party websites or their content.

No part of this publication may be reproduced, stored in a retrieval system, or transmitted in any form or by any means, electronic, mechanical, photocopying, recording, or otherwise, without written permission of the publisher. For information regarding permission, write to Scholastic Inc., Attention: Permissions Department, 557 Broadway, New York, NY 10012.

This book is a work of fiction. Names, characters, places, and incidents are either the product of the author's imagination or are used fictitiously, and any resemblance to actual persons, living or dead, business establishments, events, or locales is entirely coincidental.

ISBN 978-1-338-33884-3

10 9 8 7 6 5 4 3 2 1   20 21 22 23 24

Printed in the U.S.A.   40
First printing 2020

Book design by Baily Crawford

6

For the longest time, I thought I'd do anything to hear Isabella's voice again.

I would cut off all my hair and donate it to charity. I'd mow every lawn in the neighborhood, I'd get straight As on every test and piece of homework, I'd even eat all my vegetables at every meal.

Anything.

All I wanted was to hear her laugh again as we hid from our parents in our blanket fort, or have her braid my hair, or lie in our bedroom until way too late at night, talking about which teachers we thought were aliens or what we wanted to be when we grew up.

Isabella never got to grow up.

I thought I'd do anything to bring her back. To give her another chance at life. To have her be my sister again.

And then, with the help of my friends, we *did* bring her back . . .

. . . or at least we brought *something* back.

1

"More hot chocolate?" my mom asked from the top of the stairs.

My friends giggled. We'd probably already had enough sugar to fuel a small country, but it was cold outside and it felt like it could snow at any minute, even though it was only the beginning of October. *More hot chocolate* was a no-brainer.

"Yes, please!" I called out.

My friend Tara giggled again and hid her face behind her hands; she was just admitting which classmate she had a crush on, and my mom's timing couldn't have been worse. Mom *definitely* heard what we were talking about, but, thankfully, she didn't say anything. She just turned and went back into the kitchen to make our third pot of hot chocolate.

"I don't know," Lauren continued once the door shut. "Avery's kind of funny-looking."

"I don't care!" Tara blurted out. "What do *you* think, Maria?"

I didn't answer right away. Not because I didn't think Avery was cute. But because I hadn't really thought of Avery—or anyone—that way in a long time.

Clearly, Tara could tell where my mind was headed, because she quickly changed the subject.

"I know!" she said. "We should play a game!"

"Yeah, great idea," Lauren said. "Do you have any board games?" she asked me.

I nodded. "They're upstairs. I'll go grab them."

Tara and Lauren and I had been friends since third grade. We met playing soccer, and when it was clear none of us were very good at it, we became fast friends—mostly because we could laugh at how bad we were. Two years later, they were still the best friends I had. We'd done everything together, from water parks to sleepovers to matching Halloween costumes.

Tara was always the daring one. Passing silly notes under the teacher's nose in class. Making prank calls from the school. One time, she even hid a tiny mouse in our teacher's desk drawer. The teacher never found it, though—the mouse must have escaped.

Tara probably would have gotten us in trouble many times if not for Lauren's quick thinking. Lauren wasn't the bravest, but she was definitely the smartest of our group, and she could make teachers or parents believe anything. Most of the time, she was convincing people that Tara was innocent of something Tara most definitely did. It was never anything *bad*, really. But sometimes Tara's view of *fun* was a little too intense.

Tara and Lauren were the closest people to me in the world . . . although that still wasn't nearly as close as I'd been to Isabella. At one time, all four of us had been besties. Now it was just Tara and Lauren and me.

I tried not to dwell on this as I made my way out of the basement fort and up the stairs to the kitchen.

I'd converted the entire room of our finished basement into an awesome fort: Sheets hung between chairs and from the ceiling to make a roof, and LED lights were strung about for stars, and I plugged in some cinnamon air fresheners so it smelled like baking and not like damp mold, which it sometimes did if Mom didn't keep the dehumidifier running. Tara and Lauren had helped make it homier, adding in scarves and twinkle lights and tapestries scrounged up from their own houses. Initially, we had just built it for a night of telling ghost stories, but it was so comfortable that we didn't take it down the next day. Or the next. My mom always said we needed to take it down, but then . . .

Then Isabella passed away, and my parents knew deep down that the fort made me feel connected to her. They hadn't asked me to take it down since.

Just the thought was a spear to my heart, and I stumbled on a step and nearly fell.

"You okay?" Tara asked from below.

"Yeah," I replied. But the truth was, no, I wasn't okay. I wasn't okay at all. That's why my friends were here. They were supposed to help me forget that I wasn't okay. Because forgetting felt like the only way to feel better. School had been going for a month. That should have been enough to keep my mind off things, to help me *move forward*, just like my new guidance counselor always said.

But even though Isabella had been gone for months, I still couldn't stop thinking about her. Everything I saw or did reminded me of her. Even hanging out with my friends was different. Emptier. It used to be all four of us telling stories or playing sports or going on adventures. Isabella's absence was almost its own presence, a huge empty space none of us could fill, no matter how loud we talked or how often we laughed.

It was clear I wasn't the only one who still felt her absence. Ever since Isabella had died, my parents were like completely different people. Or at least Mom was. Dad was barely there at all.

My mom hummed away at the stove, stirring a big pot of milk and shaking in cocoa powder.

"What are you doing up here, pumpkin?" she asked. "I was going to bring the cocoa down for you."

"Gonna get some board games," I replied.

She smiled warmly. This was the first time I'd had friends over since school started, and I knew she was glad to see me actually being social. But even though she was smiling, it didn't really touch her eyes. I don't think I'd seen her truly smile since Isabella passed. Now Mom was constantly cleaning or organizing or cooking. Trying to fill up the silence left by my sister.

"Games sound fun," she said. "Just try not to stay up too late, okay?"

"We won't," I replied. Though I knew we would. Especially if we were about to drink even more hot chocolate.

She dropped her voice to a conspiratorial whisper. "Now, how spicy should we make the cocoa?"

My mom made the *best* hot chocolate. She mixed in cayenne pepper and honey and real dark chocolate and cream, so it was smooth and silky and spicy.

Isabella never liked it spicy, but I did.

I always let Isabella pick.

"Spicy," I said. I forced myself to smile.

You have to forget and move on, I thought, even though that felt like the hardest possible thing to do. Everyone said I should move on, like it was easy, like changing your clothes. But it felt like no matter how hard I tried, everything reminded me of my sister. Forgetting her seemed impossible, and besides, I loved her too much to want to forget in the first place.

"All right, then," Mom said. "You grab your games, and I'll bring these down when I'm done. I might even have some cookies hiding in the cupboard, if you're lucky . . ."

My smile turned real, and I went over and hugged her waist.

"I love you," I said.

She reached down and gave me a squeeze with one arm, her other stirring the cocoa slowly. "I love you, too," she said. "Now go have fun with your friends!"

I nodded and bounded up to my room.

The upstairs was dark, and even with the night-lights, it gave me chills. My room was at the end of the hall, past my mom and dad's—I could hear Dad in his office, watching TV. He rarely came out anymore, and when he did, he looked older than I'd ever seen him. Older even than my grandfather. I think it was part of the reason my mom kept so busy—she was trying to drown out the silence left by my dad as well. Before Isabella died, Mom and Dad would blast music and laugh at the top of their lungs or dance randomly in the living room. They were, to quote Tara, *disgustingly, cutely in love.*

It only made Dad's sudden isolation more jarring.

Even though I knew he was up there with me, the hall felt empty. Ominous. Shadows seemed to seep from around my door. I hesitated. Because right next to it, the door just slightly ajar, was Isabella's room.

I hadn't gone in there since she passed away. But I thought Mom and Dad always kept it closed? Maybe Mom had gone in to clean and didn't click it shut, and a draft had opened it?

It had to be my imagination, but as I hurried past Isabella's room, I swore I felt a cool breeze trickling down my forearms and the back of my neck. And it smelled like . . .

No, it was just my imagination.

Just a draft carrying the perfume of Isabella from her room into the hall. That had to be it. Had to.

I quickly flipped the switch on in my room and looked about. It was perfectly clean, just as I liked it. The bed made, corners tucked in tight. All my stuffed animals lined up along the pillows. My dolls in a neat row, from tallest to shortest, along the window. I went over to my closet, to the perfectly ordered clothes hanging from the rack, all arranged by color so it was a perfect rainbow when I opened the door. I loved rainbows. They made me happy.

I grabbed a step stool and took down the board games from the top shelf of my closet.

Something slipped off the top box and landed in the clothes hamper with a thump I felt in my chest.

I climbed down and set the boxes to the side. Then, with shaking hands, I went over and grabbed the upside-down photo from the hamper.

I turned it to face me—

Isabella smiled back.

Well, me and Isabella. Both of us standing in front of a fountain, our arms around each other's waist. Isabella, my twin sister, with her short black hair and dark brown skin and deep brown eyes. We each held a stuffed animal that our parents had gifted us that morning: her, a brown teddy bear, and me, a white rabbit. We even wore matching dresses, mine in white and hers in light pink.

We couldn't have been happier. Her smile was as bright as sunshine, just like mine.

Little did we know that a month after the photo was taken, I would never see her smile again.

"I'm sorry," I whispered to the photograph.

I'd whispered it a hundred thousand times before. *Sorry* didn't change anything.

Sorry didn't make her death any less my fault.

With shame clenching my heart, I gently hid the photograph in a stack of folded jeans.

"You have to move on," I told myself again.

I wiped the tears that had begun to form. I had to move on. I had to.

I couldn't bring her back.

I grabbed the games and made my way downstairs to my friends, trying my best to leave the memory of Isabella behind me.

She was everywhere. She was everywhere, yet I could never, ever get her back.

2

"Ooooh," Tara said, glancing at her watch. "Guess what time it is? It's midnight!"

"What?" I asked, looking up from the final game piece I was neatly putting back in the box. "That's impossible."

"Yeah," Lauren said, flopping back on a mound of pillows. "I thought it was like five a.m. That last game took for*ever*."

Tara threw another pillow at her.

"Yeah," she said, "but only because you kept changing your mind when it was your turn." She smiled deviously. "But you know what midnight means, don't you?"

"That it's way past bedtime?" I asked.

"No," she said, her grin widening. She reached over and grabbed her backpack. "It means the witching hour is upon us."

"Witching hour?" I asked. The very phrase made me shudder.

Tara pulled something from her bag.

"Oh no, not another game," Lauren moaned.

"Not a game," Tara said. She held the box in her lap, tilting the cover toward us. "*Definitely* not a game."

"The Mystic's Oracle," I read aloud. More chills raced over me.

I knew that Mom would *not* want that in the house. Too late now, though.

"What is it?" Lauren asked.

"It's a spirit board," Tara said. She moved aside the old game box and set the new one down between the three of us, then pulled out a large piece of thin wood covered in letters and stars. "I found it in my aunt's house. It's real old. You use it to talk to dead people." She pulled out a circular piece of clear plastic with a silver star in the middle of it, about the size of a peanut butter jar lid. It looked like the lens of a big magnifying glass.

"What if I don't want to talk to dead people?" Lauren pressed groggily. "I just wanna go to sleep. It's late."

Tara didn't say anything, but I saw her eyes flicker toward me. Even though the three of us were best friends, Tara was the only one who truly knew how much I was still hurting from Isabella's death. I'd cried on her shoulder so many times. But I hadn't told her the full truth. No one knew.

Tara thought I was just sad because I missed my sister. She didn't realize it was only worsened because of my guilt.

She placed the circular piece in the middle of the board.

"Come on, just try it," Tara said. "And keep an open mind. Midnight is when the veil between the worlds is thin and it's easier to contact the other side."

"Where'd you hear that?" Lauren asked.

Tara shrugged. "It's just common knowledge. Or are you chicken?"

"You just heard that on TV," Lauren said. But, seeing that Tara wasn't going to be dissuaded— she never was when she wanted to do something, *especially* if it was something mildly dangerous— Lauren groaned. *"Fiiiiine."*

Tara looked at me for real this time. She was waiting for my approval. I nodded. I would try this. If I could talk to Isabella, maybe I could come clean. I could clear my conscience. If I could talk to her, it meant she wasn't truly gone.

Suddenly, the basement seemed oppressive—the shadows in the corners of the fort pressed in on all sides, heavy and thick. Like the house was holding its breath.

Watching.

Waiting.

Knowing.

"Okay," Tara said. "We all put the tips of our first two fingers lightly on the oracle globe."

"The what?" Lauren asked.

"The plastic thingy," Tara replied. "Lightly. Like you're touching a butterfly wing."

"You're not supposed to touch butterfly wings," Lauren said. "If you disturb the dust on them, they'll never fly again."

Tara glared at Lauren. "Are you in or not?"

"I'm in, I'm in," Lauren said with a huge yawn.

Lauren put her fingers on the plastic piece. I shuffled closer to her and did the same. I couldn't take my eyes off the board and its old-fashioned calligraphy letters. It looked like wood grain and black paint, not some cheap printed card stock like our other board games. For some reason, the fact that it was an antique made it seem more legitimate. My fingers trembled slightly.

Was Isabella listening? Could this really work?

I almost didn't want to find out.

Now that I was facing the possibility of actually speaking to her, I was afraid of what she would say.

"Okay," Tara said seriously. More serious than I'd heard her in a long time. "I'll go first. We'll each ask a question out loud, one at a time, and the rest of us will focus on that question until we feel the oracle globe move. You're not supposed to *try* and move the globe. You need to keep a gentle touch and let the spirits work through you."

Tara put her fingers on the plastic pointer and closed her eyes.

"I call to you, spirits," she said in a hushed voice. "Come to our aid. We seek your counsel in these worldly matters."

Outside the blanket fort, a pillow fell over with a soft thump. We all jumped.

Lauren giggled, but I could tell she didn't really find it funny. She was nervous. Tara quirked open an eye. I nudged Lauren, and she stopped giggling. My skin felt like it was filled with static electricity— every single nerve was on fire. Waiting. Wanting to see what—if anything—would happen next.

Maybe it was my imagination, but the basement suddenly seemed a lot quieter.

The darkness above a lot heavier.

Despite having my closest friends beside me, my fingers began to shake.

It felt like there were more people here than just the three of us.

I could practically feel someone—or many *someones*—breathing down the back of my neck.

"I think they're here," Tara whispered. She closed her eyes again. "Okay, spirits. I ask of thee: What is the name of my secret admirer?"

We sat there for a long time. The pointer didn't move.

Lauren snorted. "Maybe you don't *have* a secret admirer, Tara."

"Shh!" Tara said.

And then the pointer began to move.

Slowly, it slid across the board, the inner star finally landing and stalling on an O.

"Oooh," Lauren said. "Maybe it's Oliver!"

"Ewww, he picks his nose in class!" I said with a giggle. The laughter felt forced, though—everything about this moment felt deadly serious.

Either the spirits were here and listening or this was all just a silly game.

"Shh!" Tara hissed, louder this time.

The pointer slid.

R

"R? Who has a name that starts with OR?" Lauren whispered with another giggle.

Y

X

A

3

"Okay, this is just stupid, this *clearly* doesn't work—it's all gibberish!" Lauren said, throwing up her hands and flopping back on her pillows. "I'm going to sleep."

Tara and I watched her shuffle over to a corner of the blanket fort, cuddling up amid the pillows and blankets. Seconds later, she was snoring.

"I can't believe her," Tara said.

"Yeah," I replied. "That was really rude."

"That, and I don't know how she fell asleep so quickly."

She sighed and looked down.

Both of us still had our fingertips pressed to the oracle.

"Did you want to have a go?" Tara whispered. "Or did you want to go to bed?"

I couldn't answer right away.

I don't think I could have taken them away if I tried. My fingertips tingled with static electricity, and it made my whole body feel alive and aware and very, very awake.

"You saw the answer it just gave," I said. "It doesn't work."

"That was because of Lauren. She doesn't believe." She looked me in the eyes. "But *you* believe. I know you do. Just like I know you . . ." She hesitated and looked down at the board. "Just like I know you have a reason to want to talk to the spirits. I brought this because I thought of you."

My heart flipped.

Of course she had been thinking of me when she brought it over. She'd done everything she could to make me feel better in the months that had followed

Isabella's death. From letting me sob while we watched movies or bringing me my favorite cookies out of the blue, she was there for me every day. Which was part of the reason I'd tried so hard to move on. I hated her seeing me like that. I hated her feeling like she had to take care of me. This, I knew, was another way of helping.

Of trying to help me move on.

Just like everyone else's efforts, I doubted this would work. But I would try anyway. For her.

I nodded gravely.

"Okay, then," Tara said. "Ask your question. I know Isabella's listening."

3

Silence settled like cold hands on my shoulders as I stared down at the oracle board.

Isabella's listening.

It was a statement I could barely bring myself to believe.

If Isabella was listening now, did it mean she'd always been listening? Did she hear me crying myself to sleep at night? Did she hear my thoughts, begging her to come back?

Did she hear my guilt? All the words I wished I'd said, rather than the silence that killed her?

I swallowed, fear and guilt burning like acid in my throat.

If she had been there, watching, listening, why had she never responded? How could this stupid piece of thin wood and plastic relay the words I'd been yearning to hear for the last few months? I was just getting my hopes up. This wasn't moving forward—this was holding on to the past.

"I don't think this is a good idea," I said. "It doesn't feel right."

And it wasn't just my worries over communicating with Isabella or not.

I couldn't shake the feeling that the three of us were not alone down here. And the more Tara and I sat in silence, the more the presence grew. Goose bumps pricked up all over my skin, and now I didn't just feel someone breathing behind me . . . I *heard* it. Hoarse and raspy, expectant, rattling like wind through jangling bones.

"If that's the case," Tara said, "why are your hands still on the pointer?"

And it was true. Even though I was afraid, my fingers were frozen to the plastic pointer between us. It sat there, motionless, taunting me. Would it answer?

And if it answered, who was the one speaking through it?

I was about to pull my hands away, when I sensed it. A sudden, light breeze, like someone had walked past. And I knew the scent that followed, deep in my bones. Isabella's shampoo. It filled my nostrils, calming me instantly.

Maybe it was my imagination, but I felt better. At least a little.

"Come on," Tara whispered. "You owe it to yourself to at least try. At worst, she doesn't respond and it's all a silly game. But at best, you get to talk to her. Wouldn't you like that? Don't you think *she* would want that?"

That question was enough to squash my doubts. Isabella definitely wouldn't have wanted me to be holding on to my sadness. She'd want me to move forward and be happy again. And if that meant communicating with her through this board and saying all the things I wished I could have said, I'd do it. Even if it didn't work. I'd have said what I wanted to say, and I could move on.

The scent of her shampoo grew stronger, and I could swear I felt her warm hands on top of mine.

"Isabella," I asked, my voice scratchy with unshed tears, "are you there?"

I held my breath. I could tell that Tara was doing the same.

For the longest time, the pointer didn't move. Seconds ticked by, turning to minutes that felt like hours as I concentrated on that round piece of plastic and internally begged for Isabella to answer. For her to respond.

In my heart, I knew that if she responded, it meant she forgave me.

I sighed after a while.

"This isn't—" I began.

The pointer moved.

Twitched.
I gasped in amazement as slowly
    inch
            by
                  inch
it moved to the top-right corner of the board. To
the word encircled by stars.

                                  YES

4

I jerked my hands back into my lap, goose bumps fresh on my skin.

"Did you do that?" I asked Tara.

She shook her head, her eyes wide.

"You have to tell me the truth," I pressed, my voice frantic. "Did you move it?"

"No," Tara said. Her own voice was breathless. "I swear. I thought you did."

"No. No way. I didn't move it."

"Then that means—" Tara gulped. "That means that Isabella is here. And she's willing to talk to us."

She looked down to the board, then back to me. "Did you want to continue?" she asked.

A part of me still didn't believe that she hadn't been moving it. How could this board communicate with Isabella when all my tears and whispered questions in bed could not? What if this was all just some elaborate hoax by Tara to get me to move on? Except that didn't seem like her. Tara liked pushing the rules and taking risks, but she wasn't mean—she would never do something to deceive me. Would she?

The worst part was, for the first time since Isabella had died, hope blossomed in my chest. Hope that I could talk to her again. That I could make things right. That everything could be okay. That hope felt even more dangerous with the belief that Tara might be behind all this.

"Maria?" Tara asked, bringing me back to the present. "We don't have to keep going if you don't want to."

I swallowed hard. The uncertainty in her voice made me think she was telling the truth. She was just as nervous about all of this as I was.

Which meant, maybe . . . maybe this was real. And if it was, I couldn't lose the opportunity to talk to my sister.

My hands shaking, I placed my fingers back on the pointer. Tara did the same.

"Isabella," I croaked. "Are you . . . are you okay?"

Once more, the pointer didn't move for a few breaths. Then, slowly, it moved away, tilting down an inch toward the bottom of the board before circling back and landing on

YES.

I gasped in relief as tears filled my eyes, making the board waver.

"Oh, Isabella, I'm so glad. I miss you so, so much."

The pointer started moving, spelling out four words that made my heart ache.

I
MISS
YOU
TOO

"Maria, this—" Tara whispered. "This is—"

"Impossible," I replied. I looked up to the lights flickering above my blanket fort. The tears flowing down my cheeks made the lights flicker and dance like they were swimming. But I didn't take my hands off the pointer. I didn't want to break the spell. I felt so torn. A part of me couldn't believe this was true. There was no way to talk to the dead. No way this was truly my sister talking to me. It had to be Tara. Had to be a trick.

Except . . .

The rest of me didn't want this to be a trick. I *wanted* to believe this was Isabella. Wanted to believe my sister was sitting behind me, her hands over mine, guiding the pointer to the words I so badly wanted to hear. I squeezed my eyes shut. Another inhale, another whiff of her shampoo. I could believe it was her. I could believe she was here.

"I wish you were here," I whispered.

I wish you'd never left me.

"Maria," Tara said, and maybe it was my imagination, but it sounded like she was scared. Why should she be scared? My sister was here, with us. Just like she should be. A year ago, it would have been the four of us down here, all of us friends, all of us giggling. Maybe it could be like that again. Maybe . . .

That's when I realized the pointer was moving again.

I looked down to catch it spelling out another sentence, the pointer hovering just briefly over the letters it selected.

I
C
A
N
B
E

"What?" I asked. She could be with me. She could be back with us. It could be like it used to be. "How?"

"Maria, are you doing this?"

"No. Are you?"

She shook her head. "Maybe we shouldn't—"

But the pointer was moving again, faster now, and Tara went silent as she watched, her mouth hanging open.

I
N
V
I
T
E
M
E
I
N

"Okay, that's it," Tara said. She threw her hands up in the air. The pointer went still. "Maria, this isn't right."

"What do you mean it isn't right?" I asked. "This was your idea in the first place—you can't just give up now. It's Isabella! She's here! We can get her back. It's her, I know it is!"

"But how do we know?" she asked.

Her question threatened to deflate my tiny balloon

of hope. No, it had to be Isabella. Had to. Who else could it be? The scent of shampoo was heavy in my nostrils, and I knew without a doubt it was her.

"It is," I replied. "I know it is. She was my sister! I know what it feels like when she's around. It's her. It has to be."

Tara shook her head. "Maybe it was a mistake to bring this out," she said. "I mean, maybe that *was* Isabella. But it's dangerous. Who knows what will happen if you invite her in?"

I'd have my sister back, I wanted to say. I didn't, though. I hung my head.

My fingers still rested on the board.

Tara shifted and came over to me, putting her hands on my shoulders.

"I'm sorry," she said. "But this doesn't feel right. We should stop. It's late, and I don't want us to do anything we'd regret."

"What do you mean? What would we regret? This is Isabella, not some monster."

She hesitated and looked at the board as if it were a live snake.

"But we don't know that," she said softly. "I know you're not supposed to invite spirits in."

"But this was your idea!"

"I know . . . I know, but now it's my idea to stop. At least for tonight. We can try again in the morning, okay?" She looked around uncomfortably. "I don't know. This feels wrong. We're in over our heads."

She stood.

"I'm gonna run to the bathroom. Then we should probably go to sleep." She looked over to Lauren, as if looking for support from our sleeping friend. Lauren snored and turned over.

"Okay," I said. "Okay, we can stop."

Tara crouched and made her way out of the fort.

It was only when the curtain fell shut behind her and I was alone—sort of—that I realized my hands were still glued to the oracle board pointer. And, as if a current of electricity were buzzing through me, they tingled with excitement.

"Isabella," I whispered. "Are you still there?"

I didn't move a muscle.

I didn't shift my fingers an inch.
But the pointer twitched.
    Moved.

                                        YES

5

I looked up and around. As if expecting Tara to jump from the shadows and say this was all a prank. But she was gone, and Lauren was snoring, and the pointer definitely, *definitely* moved on its own.

I knew Tara would freak out if she knew I was continuing—especially without her—but I also knew this defied all logic and it felt like if I didn't act now, the moment would slip away and I'd lose my ability to talk with Isabella for good. This couldn't wait until morning. She was here. Now. And I couldn't guarantee that she would be here when I woke up. All of this felt like a dream. I couldn't risk the reality dawn brought.

"Isabella," I whispered. "About what happened . . . I just wanted to say. I mean, I know it doesn't mean anything. Not after . . . But I'm so, so sorry. Can you . . . ?" The words choked in my throat. The answer I didn't want. The truth I couldn't bear. "Can you forgive me?"

The pointer moved. Faster than it had before.

Y
O
U
R
F
A
U
L
T

The words hit like a stab in the heart; fresh tears welled in my eyes. This time, not from relief, but from guilt.

I forced down the memory of that day, of the terrible moment when I lost my sister. I forced it down, but that didn't stop the fresh surge of dark emotion within me.

Because she was right. She was right.

"I know," I whispered, my words half a sob. "I know, and I'm sorry. I want to make it right. How can I make it right?"

Faster the pointer moved, guiding my hands so quickly it nearly pulled out from under my fingertips.

I
N
V
I
T
E
M
E
I
N

The words echoed in my head.

A small, rational voice inside me—one that sounded an awful lot like Lauren—said that I should do no such thing.

The other, louder voice, the one that was most certainly my own, said that I owed Isabella this much. And more.

I had to try and make it right. Even though it was something that could never be made right.

I had to try.

Had to.

"Okay," I whispered. *I invite you in.*

6

I expected something momentous to happen.

For Isabella to appear in a halo of golden light, shimmery and angelic. Or perhaps to feel her hands on my shoulders and her whisper in my ear, saying she forgave me.

There was only silence.

Silence, and the slight tingle on the back of my neck, a cold breeze I wasn't entirely sure was just a draft.

I strained my ears, hoping to hear her telltale laughter—

and nearly jumped out of my skin when the

basement door opened and someone creaked down the steps. The fort curtain opened, and Tara stuck her head inside.

"What are you doing?" she asked. She was looking at my hands, which were still firmly placed on the pointer.

I pulled my hands back to my lap, my face flushing with guilt.

"Nothing," I lied.

"Were you still trying to talk to her?" she asked. She came into the fort and sat down beside me. She leaned her shoulder against mine, comfortingly. "You know it only works with two people, right?"

Does it?

I nodded glumly. My words were caught in my throat—even if I could have spoken, I didn't think I would want to. Because the pointer had moved with only one person. And I had done the one thing Tara warned me not to do.

Yet Isabella hadn't appeared.

Had I just been imagining things?

Maybe I'd been forcing the pointer to move

without realizing it, because some deep, secret part of me had known what I wanted to hear. Or what I dreaded to hear.

Tara clearly noticed my confusion, but she must have mistaken my sadness for defeat.

"Come on," she said. "Let's get some sleep."

"Okay." My words came out in a croak.

I helped her put the board and pointer back in their box, and we both settled into our sleeping bags. I reached out and turned off the string lights sparkling above, casting the basement into a gentle darkness lit by a few night-lights.

I closed my eyes and tried to push away thoughts of the oracle board. It hadn't worked. It couldn't have worked.

Otherwise, Isabella would have shown herself.

Otherwise, I would have known for sure that she was there.

I had to move on.

And that meant I had to stop telling myself she could still hear me. I had to stop letting myself get swept away in fantasy. I had to let go of the guilt of what had happened that terrible day.

Isabella was dead, and no matter what I or anyone else did, she wasn't coming back.

"I wish you were here," I whispered to myself, quiet enough that Tara couldn't hear.

And maybe it was my imagination, but I swore, as sleep drifted in, that deep in the darkness I heard my sister's voice:

"I *am*."

7

In my dreams, Isabella was alive.

Her laughter rang through the basement, mingling with my own. Upstairs, I heard my mom and dad cleaning—the vacuum was roaring and music was playing. But down here, Isabella and I were a world away. In our combined imagination, the basement was transformed into a deep tropical jungle. The blanket-fort sheets hanging from the rafters were draped vines, and serpents and jaguars prowled in the shadows.

Those vines could be hiding anything, including the dreaded evil leech . . .

"I'm coming for you!" Isabella yelled out.

She burst through the sheets, fully enveloped in an army green sleeping bag, with only her head poking out the top. She hopped over toward me, and I yelped, hopping back and nearly tripping from my own navy blue sleeping bag.

"The evil leech is starving!" she yelled gleefully. "And she's hungry for giant slugs!"

I yelled out in a fit of giggles as I thumped over a pillow and landed in a pile of comforters. I tried to squirm away, but I couldn't move fast enough, and moments later, Isabella flopped down on top of me with a soft *thwump*.

"Got you!" she called triumphantly. She started flopping around me like a fish, poking me with her hands through the sleeping bag, making *nom nom nom* sounds as she pretended to devour me. I kept giggling, laughing so hard I could barely breathe. It tickled, and with both my arms trapped in the bag, I didn't have a chance to fend her off.

"Can't breathe!" I finally gasped between fits of wheezing laughter. "Can't! Breathe!"

She didn't stop tickling me, though. And with every second, she was getting heavier, pressing down harder, and the tickling was starting to hurt. I twisted around, trying to get out from under her but only managing to twist the bag so I couldn't see out of the opening anymore. Blackness covered me. A stifling, heavy blackness.

"Isabella!" I gasped, panic starting to lace through my glee. "I can't breathe!"

Heavier she became, until my laughter turned to frantic gasps and the bag seemed to constrict around me, pulling tighter and tighter, pressing the air from my lungs as a hundred invisible hands poked into my sides. Darkness dragged me down, and I knew if I didn't escape soon, I never would.

Even though I was no longer laughing, Isabella was.

"Please!" I gasped.

"*Please!*" she squealed back. "I want you to know how it feels, Maria. To not be able to breathe. To not be able to scream."

Heavier.

And heavier.

The bag squeezed tighter

and *tighter*.

I couldn't breathe in.

Couldn't push her off.

Stars exploded in the blackness as my thoughts ricocheted around one realization.

I was going to die.

Isabella was going to kill me.

"I want you to know how it feels to be afraid."

The stars in my eyes grew brighter. Condensed into two blinding points of light.

Headlights

coming straight toward me

and as the car careened out of the darkness,

as Isabella's laughter howled with the car's panicked horn,

I was finally able to gasp.

I screamed—

8

—and woke up tangled in my sleeping bag.

Darkness swam around me, and the moment I jolted upright so, too, did Tara and Lauren. Tara's eyes were wide.

"What's wrong?" she asked, quickly clambering to my side.

"I—I just—" I gasped and looked around, as if I was expecting a car to hurtle out of the walls and smash into us. Then, when reality finally sunk in and I realized I was safe and awake and in my basement, and not in the middle of the road, I flopped back to my pillows and closed my eyes. "Bad dream," I finished.

I peeked open one eye. Tara was looking at me with a concerned expression on her face. She could tell when I was lying, but I was telling the truth, right? I'd just had a nightmare. And yes, it was about Isabella, which was strange, since in all my previous dreams, she'd been kind. But it was still just a dream.

What could I expect after staying up so late drinking lots of sugar and trying to talk to my dead sister?

Trying? But you did *talk to her. You invited her in.*

The thought made my heart leap. I pushed myself up to sitting and looked over to where the oracle board lay in its box. In the light of day, it seemed like a stupid toy. I could even see the price sticker in the corner. It might have been old, but it was still something you could buy in a store. There were thousands of them made. Millions. It couldn't talk to the dead. Otherwise, everyone would be doing it and no one would mourn anyone ever again.

Lauren's voice jolted me back to reality.

"We should probably get going," Lauren said, looking at her phone. "It's already ten o'clock, and Mom wants me to help her clean this morning. Blech."

"Wait, really?" I asked. "I can't believe we slept in that long." Though down here, with all the lights low, it was impossible to tell what time it was. But now that I was listening, I thought I heard my mom walking around upstairs.

"We were up pretty late," Tara replied, sharing a knowing glance with me.

"How late?" Lauren asked. She stood and stretched, yawning deeply. "Did you, you know, make contact?"

Another knowing look between Tara and me.

"No," I said quickly, before Tara could say anything. I didn't want to freak Lauren out, or to admit to Tara that we *had* made contact with my sister and I'd secretly invited her into my home. It felt like admitting to a big mistake, one I didn't want to own up to, to either of my friends.

"Yeah, the thing didn't work," Tara continued. "No wonder Mom had stuffed it in the back of the closet."

I nodded along, but that didn't stop a frightening question from squirming through my mind: What if Tara's mom had been trying to hide it, to keep everyone else safe?

THUD THUD THUD.

I squeaked and quickly covered my mouth, but Lauren caught the noise and giggled.

"Who wants pancakes?" Mom called out.

Tara, Lauren, and I looked at one another.

"Well," Lauren said, "maybe just one. Cleaning can wait."

"Cleaning can always wait," I said with a forced smile.

We made our way toward the steps, with me in the lead. Mom had gone back into the kitchen—probably to start serving the pancakes—leaving the door wide open.

"Do you think I can have chocolate syrup on mine?" Lauren asked.

"How can you want more chocolate?" Tara asked incredulously. "You had like five cups of cocoa last night!"

"I'm sure you can," I said, looking back to smile at her.

Then I turned to the door, wondering what I was going to have on my own pancakes, when the door slammed shut in my face with a bang.

9

I nearly leaped out of my skin.

If not for Tara's quick reflexes—she instantly
threw out her hands to stop me from jumping
backward—I might have toppled into my friends.

For a moment, I couldn't move. I just stood
there, my nose only inches from the basement door
and my heart thudding so loud in my ears that
it took me a while to realize Tara and Lauren
were talking. Their voices sounded far away, like
they were coming from the bottom of a well or my
ears were stuffed with cotton. Distantly, I could feel

their hands on my shoulders, holding me upright through the shock.

Not just from the door nearly hitting my face. But from the unmistakable scent that brushed past. It smelled like . . . No, it couldn't be.

"Maria?" Lauren asked, patting me on the shoulder. "Maria, are you okay?"

"What was that?" Tara asked. "What happened?"

"I don't know," I muttered. I stared at the door in shock.

No one had been on the other side. Only Mom and maybe Dad were home—we didn't have pets or anything. And it's not like either of my parents would have been rude enough to slam the door in my face.

Plus—in that brief glance I had of the door— no one had been standing there. No one could have shut the door.

"Maybe it was a draft?" Lauren offered.

It was most definitely *not* a draft. Could it have been Isabella, making her presence known?

Why would she be so violent?

My dream flickered back through my mind. Her angry laughter, her rough words, saying she wanted me to suffer, to know how she had felt. That wasn't like my sister, and I couldn't convince myself it was all just my overactive imagination. Something didn't feel right . . .

"Come on," Tara urged, breaking me from my thoughts. "I don't want to be down in the basement any longer. It's creepy."

She moved past me and opened the door, stepping into the late-morning sunlight. It opened easily, and just as expected, there was no one and no thing behind it. Lauren followed quickly behind Tara.

"Aren't you coming?" Tara asked.

My feet felt glued to the steps.

I didn't know why, but I looked back once more. Toward the blanket fort.

And I swore I saw a shadow move.

The shadow of a young girl. There for a heartbeat, then gone.

No. No, it was just the twinkle lights, just a trick of my imagination.

So why did my imagination swear that it smelled Isabella's shampoo?

"Yeah," I said. "I'm coming."

I followed them out and toward the kitchen.

I made sure to securely latch the basement door behind me.

It didn't feel like enough.

10

My appetite was completely gone when we stepped into the kitchen. Even though it smelled amazing— warm maple syrup, fresh pancakes sizzling on the griddle, and a bowl of cut fruit—the slammed door had twisted my gut into knots. We helped ourselves to pancakes and fruit, Tara and Lauren giggling as they heaped their plates. Mom walked up behind me while I was picking out pieces of fruit.

"Not hungry?" she asked.

I shrugged. Tara and Lauren were already sitting down, talking about some show they'd been watching. How were they not freaking out about the door? Were they really content to believe it was just a draft?

"Let me guess," Mom said, putting her hands on my shoulders. "You were up too late because of all the sugar and then didn't sleep well."

I nodded, because it was sort of, almost the truth.

"Well, then, it's just vegetables and juice for you today! And a nap."

I groaned. "Mommm."

She laughed and kissed the top of my head. But then she paused, her hands tense on my shoulders.

"Did you—?" she began, but she cut herself off.

"What?" I asked. My heart started to hammer. *How did she know what we did? How did she know?*

"Did you change your shampoo?" she asked softly. So soft even I could barely hear it.

"No," I said. My heart dropped to my toes. "Why?"

"It . . . never mind."

She sniffed, and when I looked up at her, I realized it was because she was sniffing back tears.

"I'm going to take some pancakes up to your father," she said. Then she stepped away and busied herself with pancakes.

It was only after I sat at the table beside my friends that I realized what it was that Mom had meant. What it could have been that made her cry.

She had smelled it, too.

Isabella's shampoo.

I sat down beside my friends and picked at my food. I made sure to be facing the basement door. Just in case.

Even though she was holding her conversation with Lauren, I noticed that Tara kept sneaking glances at her phone. Was she reading the news?

I looked over, but Tara quickly turned off the screen so I couldn't see what it was, her cheeks slightly flushed.

"How's your dad doing?" Lauren asked quietly, drawing my attention from Tara.

It was the one question I didn't know how to answer. It was almost like when we lost Isabella, we had lost Dad, too. Mom said he was just overcome with grief, that he felt responsible. That he couldn't face reality. He rarely came out of his office.

The one time I had peeked in the door, he'd been on his computer, editing old pictures of Isabella and me. He was a photographer, so it wasn't unusual for him to spend a lot of time up there, but the new isolation had both Mom and me worried.

At times, it was easy to forget he was there at all. When he *did* show himself, he looked much older, with gray in his hair and dark circles under his eyes and a shake to his hand.

Mom said it would just take time.

I could tell that she was only trying to make me feel better, and that she didn't really believe it. But I played along. I wasn't the only one in the family who needed to be comforted.

"He's getting better," I said. "We watched a movie together a few nights ago. He even made popcorn."

"I'm glad to hear it," Lauren replied softly.

I didn't tell her that he had left halfway through the movie, in tears.

I'd heard him say that Isabella would have liked the movie, as he made his way upstairs.

"Yeah," I said. "Things are almost back to normal."

Except I knew they weren't. Not really. They never could be. Isabella was gone.

Moreover, whatever was happening was definitely not normal. I just wished I could figure out if it was Isabella reaching out, or my tired imagination, or something else entirely.

A cold, scared part of me worried—no, *knew*—that it was the last.

||

After breakfast, even though it was the last place I wanted to be, Tara and Lauren and I went down and cleaned the basement a little bit. Mom must have eaten her breakfast with Dad, because she hadn't come back down. That was probably for the best—I didn't want her asking any more questions I didn't have an answer to, like why it smelled like I was using Isabella's shampoo, or why I hadn't slept last night.

We kept the basement door open and all the lights on, and Lauren played some music on her phone.

We didn't talk about the slamming door. Instead, Lauren and Tara packed their clothes and picked up mugs and snack wrappers, singing along to the music. I was in the fort, folding the sleeping bags we had slept in and trying not to remember my nightmare, when one of the blanket walls fell down on top of me.

I yelped in fright and quickly detangled myself, immediately thinking I was under attack by a vengeful ghost. But when the blanket fell to my feet, the only person near was Lauren, staring wide-eyed at me.

"I'm sorry," she said quickly. "I didn't think I was anywhere near it!"

"It's fine," I said, my heart racing.

"Here," Tara said, coming over with a chair to step on, "I'll help you put it back up."

Together, the three of us draped the blanket over one of the many lines of yarn stretched across the ceiling. Months ago, when Isabella and I had realized we wanted to keep the fort up full-time, we'd set up an elaborate system of strings and hangers and clothespins, stretching them from one side of the basement to the other. Dad had helped us reach the taller places. When it was done, we could hang the blankets and change the size and shape of the fort, as well as drape all the lights. Just the memory made my breath catch. I could practically hear Dad and Isabella laughing as he hoisted her up to hang this very blanket.

Tears welled in my eyes, but I managed to wipe them away before anyone noticed.

"I promise I didn't mean to knock it down," Lauren said.

For a moment, I couldn't understand why she was so apologetic. Then I remembered how I'd reacted when she'd suggested, weeks ago, that maybe we should take the fort down. She said it was because it made her claustrophobic, but I knew the real reason was that it reminded her of Isabella. I'd practically yelled at her, and she'd gone home in tears. Even though I'd apologized a ton after, I knew she remembered it well.

"It's okay," I said. "It was an accident."

But was it?

I knew Lauren hadn't done it—at least, not on purpose—so what if another presence had been at work? What if Isabella was trying to reach out?

We went back to cleaning, and I didn't catch another glimpse of the girl's shadow, or smell Isabella's shampoo. *Had* I just been making it all up? It was easy to believe with all the lights on and pop music playing.

Maybe you should try again? a small voice inside me whispered.

I glanced at the oracle board and wondered if I could ask Tara to leave it behind without her getting suspicious. Wondered if maybe I could drop a pillow on top of it so she would forget it.

If I hadn't actually made contact with my sister last night, maybe I could if I tried again.

And if I *had* . . . I would have to find a way to keep talking to Isabella, right? What if she was just floating around the house, trying to speak but unable to say anything without the magic of the board? I needed to reach out to her, needed to—

No, came a more rational voice, echoing the

words I'd been telling myself for weeks: *You have to move on.*

Before I could decide one way or another, Tara tucked the oracle into her bag, and I knew that there was no way I could ask.

Lauren left first—she lived across town, and her parents picked her up—but Tara stayed behind. She lived just down the street, which meant we got to hang out almost every day. We escaped to my bedroom and flopped down on my bed.

"About last night," she said.

I tried to look suddenly interested in the tassels on my throw pillow.

"What about it?"

She hesitated.

"I heard you," she said after a moment. I glanced up—she was looking out the window. "When I was coming back from the bathroom. I heard you. You were talking to someone."

My heart began to race along with my thoughts. She had heard me talking to Isabella. What had she overheard? Should I lie? Tell her I was talking to

Lauren? One look at her told me she already knew the truth. Like Isabella, Tara was one of the few people I could never lie to. Even if I tried, she would see right through it.

I lowered my head. Now, in the light of day, admitting that I thought I'd made contact with my dead sister seemed stupid.

"I thought . . . I thought she had reached out," I whispered.

"Please tell me you didn't invite anything in," she said. The frantic tone of her voice made me look up at her. Her eyes were wide as she stared at me, as if trying to see past my secrets. "Please tell me you didn't."

"Why not?"

"Because," Tara said, and her voice actually squeaked, "it's dangerous."

"Dangerous?" I asked, my own panic rising. "Then why did you bring the board in the first place?"

"Because I didn't know!" she burst out. She smacked her hands over her mouth and looked around, but if either of my parents heard the out-burst, they didn't acknowledge it. "I didn't know," she continued in a harsh whisper. "But I woke up this morning and couldn't stop thinking about what the board asked us to do. So I looked it up online, and, and . . ."

"And what?!"

"And I've been reading stories, Maria," she said. "Terrible stories. Just . . . just tell me that you didn't invite anything in and it's all okay."

"What sort of stories?" I asked. My heart thudded in my ears, pounding in rhythm with the awful truth hammering in my thoughts: *I invited it in. I invited it in.*

Tara swallowed. And even though it was the middle of the day and fairly warm in my room, with the sunshine pouring through the windows, she grabbed a blanket from the foot of the bed and wrapped it around herself, shivering.

"Well," she said, "generally speaking, no nice spirit asks to be invited in. It's usually just evil ghosts that ask for that."

"How do you know?"

"Because once you invite a ghost in, you can't get rid of it. The spirits of your loved ones can just kind of hover around you without needing to be invited in, I guess. But the bad ones need your permission."

"What happens if they're invited in?"

She shuddered.

"All sorts of terrible things," she said. "I had to stop reading. It was giving me a stomachache."

"Tell me."

"You don't want to hear."

"*Tell me.*"

"Fine," she said with a sigh. "Once you invite a bad ghost in, they make your life miserable. There was a ton of stories about families who were haunted. Furniture moved around. Terrible visions or monsters in the hallways. Nightmares. That sort of thing. Sometimes they tried having someone remove the ghost—which never worked—but most of the time they just moved out. Though some stories said that the ghosts would follow their victims wherever they went."

"But why? What would the ghost want?"

She dropped her voice. "No one really knows. Because the ghosts are evil? Maybe they just want to hurt everyone who's alive. Maybe they like making mortal lives miserable. Or maybe . . ."

"Maybe?"

"Well, in the more extreme cases . . . Sometimes, the family was haunted or scared so badly, they all died."

Silence filled the room at her words, along with a heavy dread I couldn't shake.

"They died?" I finally asked.

"Yeah," she replied. "I didn't look into the details. But it seemed to happen a lot."

I could barely hear her response, though. All I could hear were my own stupid words last night, inviting whatever it was into my house.

What if Tara was right, and it had been some evil spirit? What if it wanted to hurt me? Or my family?

"But like I said, it doesn't matter," Tara said, nudging me gently. "Because you weren't silly enough to invite anything in after I left."

She raised an eyebrow at me. I could tell it was a

question, just as I could tell the answer she wanted to hear.

Well, no reason to make her worry.

"Of course not," I lied.

"Good," she replied. She settled back on the bed as if that were answer enough. It made me feel even guiltier—not only had I done what I shouldn't, but she trusted me so much that she didn't question me. Apparently, I *could* lie to her without her noticing. Or else she didn't want to see the truth.

I didn't either.

I swallowed hard. I wanted to change the subject, but I had to know.

"Why did you bring it?" I asked. "Even if you didn't know it was dangerous. Why did you think we would want to play?"

She shrugged. "Because I didn't think it would work. I figured we wouldn't get a response, and then you would know for sure that Isabella had moved on to a better place, and you'd be at peace."

"I am," I lied again. "At least, I will be." I thought of what my mom said about Dad's grieving. "In time."

Tara reached out and patted my shoulder consolingly.

"Well, you know I'm here for you no matter what. But I think next time I come over, I'll leave the spirit board behind."

My stomach clenched at the thought. That was it, then. The door between me and Isabella was truly closed. I'd never hear her voice again, or read her words.

I just had to hope that I hadn't actually invited a spirit in. And then we could leave all this behind us.

"Yeah," I said, forcing down the tears that threatened to give me away. "That's probably for the best."

12

We spent the rest of the morning switching between playing and helping each other out with our homework. We sat at the foot of my bed, surrounded by books and papers and stuffed animals. My stuffed rabbit leaned against me, propped beside my book.

I was trying to read, but I couldn't focus. I could only think of the oracle board sticking out of Tara's bag in the corner of my room, and the strange messages I'd received in the night, and the terrible warning that Tara had relayed. Had I really invited Isabella in? Or had that all been part of my imagination?

Or, worse—was it something different altogether? Something *evil*?

Suddenly, I heard a yelp in the hallway, along with the forceful shut of a door. Tara and I both glanced up from the books we were reading. Mom appeared in the doorway moments later, hands on her hips and her face stony. She stood right beside Tara's open bag, the oracle board clearly visible.

I didn't want her to see it.

I didn't want her to ask questions.

She didn't look down at the bag, though. Her eyes were speared on me.

"Did you open her door?" she demanded.

"What?" I asked.

"You heard me. Did you open your sister's door? You know you're not supposed to go in there. Not after . . ." She choked on the rest of whatever she was going to say and just stared at me, flustered. I could feel Tara shrinking away at my side.

"I—I didn't. I swear."

"It was wide open," she said. "If I find out you've been going in there and messing with her things . . ."

But she didn't finish her sentence. She huffed and turned around, storming down the hall.

"What was that all about?" Tara asked when Mom was back downstairs.

"Mom doesn't want us going into Isabella's room," I whispered.

"Why?"

I shrugged. It made me uncomfortable. I knew it was because—so long as Isabella's room was kept exactly as she'd left it—we could all pretend that she would come back someday. But that wasn't something I could say to Tara. It felt too sad. In more ways than one.

Tara looked back to her reading. I tried to go back to mine. But the awkwardness in the air lingered like a cloud. How had Isabella's door been opened? Was it another strange draft? Or had Tara opened it as some sort of practical joke? What if all this was some sort of setup: the oracle board and the ghost stories and the shampoo smell and the open door? What if it was all just some elaborate plan by Tara?

But why would she do something like that?

It was the only rational explanation, but it also didn't make any real sense. I could trust Tara, couldn't I?

Try as I might, I couldn't focus, couldn't stop glancing at the oracle board, my fingers itching—I wanted to try again. Wanted to reach out and see if maybe a spirit was responsible for all these strange events, and why. I tried to only look at the board when Tara was focused on her reading. I didn't want her asking questions. Downstairs, I could hear Mom cleaning, the vacuum buzzing loudly. Which was just one more thing that felt wrong; normally, she only cleaned with music blaring.

After Mom's angry departure, my bedroom seemed tense. Maybe I should put on some music? But Tara said she couldn't read with music going. She said it made it hard to concentrate. What was worse, I thought I caught the sound of crying in the hall, coming from Dad's office. Maybe he'd found a particularly emotional photo . . .

The minutes passed in an awkward silence, until

Tara's phone buzzed. She picked it up and read the text.

"Dang it," she grumbled. She typed something back and looked at me. "Mom wants to go grocery shopping. Says she's getting into the car now."

"No!" I yelped.

Tara's eyebrows rose.

"It's just . . . I was hoping we could watch a movie later."

It was a lame excuse, and we both knew it. The truth was, I wasn't certain if I didn't want her to leave because I didn't want to be alone, or because I hadn't yet figured out a way to get the oracle board. I only knew one thing—I needed to try talking to the spirit again. If it was Isabella, I couldn't stay silent.

And if it wasn't . . .

Well, if it wasn't Isabella, I needed to figure out who or what it was, and how to get rid of it.

Just as I was looking at the board, trying to figure out what to say to get Tara to leave it behind without raising any questions, movement caught the corner of my eye.

Next to my book. Next to *me*.

My stuffed rabbit's head

    slowly

        moved.

I stared at it in horror as it turned to face me.

    As its black eyes turned a violent, burning red.

    As a terrifying giggle echoed from its unmov-

        ing string mouth. A giggle that sounded

        an awful lot like Isabella's.

    The giggling filled my ears—so loud, so loud—

and then

        the screech of a car horn, the car horn

        as Isabella looked over, far too late,

        right before—

"Mom's here," Tara said, leaping to her feet and jolting me from the vision. She ran over to the window and waved. Her mom honked once more in response. I looked from her to the rabbit, whose head hadn't moved and whose eyes were once more black beads. The only proof that it had ever done anything strange was the cold sweat that had broken over my skin.

What in the world was going on?

"I'll text you later tonight," Tara said. She came over and gave me a hug, then pulled back and looked at me. "Are you okay?"

"Yeah," I said. I forced myself to make eye contact, to push my fear down. Now I *really* didn't want her to go. But I couldn't say anything, couldn't tell her I was scared. If I did, I'd have to admit what I'd done last night. "Fine. Was just lost in the reading and the horn startled me. That's all."

"Okay," she said. Clearly, she didn't believe me, but she wasn't about to keep her mom waiting. Mrs. Rose could be very impatient. "See ya tomorrow?"

I nodded.

I didn't get up from the floor as she grabbed her bag and left. I watched her go. Rather, I watched the oracle board go.

And when I looked back to the stuffed rabbit, my gut twisted with the question of what she might have left behind.

13

I didn't want to stay in my room. Not after watching the rabbit's head move, not after reliving the terrible moment when Isabella had lost her life. After watching Tara drive off from my upstairs window, I went down to the living room, watching TV while Mom cleaned in angry silence. Dad stayed upstairs in his office. I tried to force myself to forget about everything that had happened since last night, to convince myself it had all just been a bad dream. *This* was real—the TV, Mom cleaning quietly, and Dad upstairs, hiding away from the world. It was the new normal, and even though I didn't like it, that didn't mean I could go around making up ghost stories to distract me from reality.

And yet . . . when I flipped on the television and the station turned to one of my favorite shows, a pang of sadness shot through my chest.

This had been the show Isabella and I watched on Saturday afternoons.

We'd hang out here, cuddled up on the sofa, while Mom and Dad cleaned and played their music way too loudly, often singing at the top of their lungs, or dancing in front of the TV so badly that Isabella and I would break into laughter, yelling at them to move, *move*.

Move!

I should have yelled it. Should have said something. But the word had caught in my throat, and now I was doomed to spend the rest of my life sitting on the sofa alone while my mom moved about in silence and Dad pretended he didn't exist.

Tears welled in my eyes. I flipped to another channel. A show I'd never watched before.

Everything was new.

Everything was new, and I hated it. Even this new show.

An hour or so later, Mom poked her head into the living room. I expected her to yell at me for having the TV too loud, but instead, her voice was soft.

"Maria?" she asked. "Can you go clean your bedroom before lunch, please? And bring your laundry down to the basement."

I swallowed hard, new fear lodged in my chest at the thought of going back to my room and facing the rabbit, then looked outside. I was being ridiculous. Sunlight shone through the trees, and birds sang loudly—it was too nice a day for anything bad to happen. It was impossible to think that something dark and supernatural was going on when the world outside was so bright. Especially something as silly as, what? A ghost-possessed stuffed animal?

I turned off the TV and made my way upstairs.

Maybe it was my imagination, but I swore it got colder with every footstep.

When I reached the top hallway, I heard laughter.

Isabella's laughter? I froze, straining my ears. But after a moment, I realized it was just coming from the TV in my dad's office. He must be watching a sitcom. I shook my head. *You're being ridiculous*, I repeated.

Chastising myself for letting my imagination get the better of me, I made my way to my room.

As I passed by Isabella's room, a cold draft billowed from her slightly open door, making me shudder. I paused. My pulse quickened as I looked back toward my dad's office. Mom was now vacuuming downstairs, and Dad's door was closed.

Closed, just as her door should have been.

I knew it had been shut. Not even Mom went in here on her cleaning days. Isabella's room was sacred. Undisturbed.

It was the last of her living memory.

Her door creaked open, just a little bit more, as another cool breeze swept past. Something seemed to pull me forward. Curiosity, maybe. Or maybe it was the ache of missing her, of wanting to be close to her. Of wondering if I had called her back, and she was waiting for me inside this room.

I knew I should have just closed her door and gone to my room to clean it. Like Mom had asked.

I didn't.

Instead, after making double sure the coast was clear, I carefully opened Isabella's door the rest of the way and slipped inside.

14

Isabella's room was cold. I mean, Mom always kept the house kind of cool in the fall to conserve energy, but even with the heating ducts in Isabella's room closed off, the air felt chillier than it should have. I could practically see my breath in the thin light filtering through the curtains as I quietly shut her door behind me.

A crypt. That was it. The room felt like a crypt.

I stood in the doorway, unwilling to move but unable to leave, staring around at Isabella's room in morbid curiosity.

I had only been in here once since her death.

Once, and that had been days after she'd passed away, days after Mom and Dad had come in and cleaned and arranged everything so it looked like she was just away at school, like she could come back at any moment. Everything was tidy and in its place.

The books were all lined up on the shelf, beside trophies from spelling bees and soccer. Her dolls were all neat atop her dresser, each wearing a fancy dress, lined up beside her photographs—some were copies of the photos I had on my own dresser. Her bed was well made, the covers tight like in a hotel room, with her stuffed animals all arranged by her pillows, and her prize teddy bear—the one she'd gotten the same day I got my rabbit—in the center.

Gently, trying my best not to make the floorboards squeak, I made my way over to the dresser and picked up one of the photos. It was one I didn't have in my room. It was her and me, a few months ago. It was taken right after the last day of school, on our back patio. Isabella and I were holding hands, frozen mid-leap in the air, while old homework fluttered around us like snow. It was Dad's idea, and it had taken him four tries to get the shot right. Which just meant we'd had to jump up and down and throw our homework in the air four times. By the end of the photo shoot, we'd been laughing so hard we couldn't breathe.

I can't breathe—

I pushed the memory away as I set down the photo, but I couldn't get the words to fade, not entirely.

Tears welled up in the corners of my eyes.

"It's my fault," I whispered to the photo. "It's all my fault you're gone."

"*It* is *your fault,*" came a voice. One frighteningly familiar. The same voice I'd heard earlier—Isabella's, but meaner.

I froze.

And looked over to see the dolls turn their heads
    one
    by
    one
        to stare at me, their porcelain eyes boring
        into my soul.

The one nearest to me smiled, its painted lips quirking up menacingly as she raised a hand and pointed at me. Her eyes began glowing red.

"And we will make you pay for what you did. You hear us, Maria? You. Will. Pay!"

I jumped back and stumbled, falling flat on the floor.

Giggling surrounded me, and I watched, terrified, as the dolls on the dresser floated up into the air, hovering over me like bats.

"You let us in, Maria," the dolls said, their voices scratchy and piercing. **"You let us in, and now you will never get away from your guilt!"**

The dolls cackled and dove toward me, their tiny hands reaching out to claw out my eyes.

I raised my hands to protect my face, screaming.

"Maria!" called my father. "What in the world are you doing in here?"

Tears filled my eyes and my lungs burned, but when I lowered my arms, I found my dad standing in the doorway and the dolls neatly arranged on the dresser, right where they belonged.

"I—I—"

"You know you're not supposed to be in here," he said. "Your mom just told you off for leaving the door open earlier."

His voice took on a gentler tone as he stepped in. Even in silhouette, he looked older. More tired. Isabella's death had impacted him most of all. He thought it was his fault. Even though the dolls were right—it was mine. It was mine.

He knelt down at my side and helped me to sitting. I couldn't stop looking around, waiting for the dolls to attack. Waiting for something nightmarish to happen.

Nothing did.

And I knew that asking him if he'd seen anything would just make him worry. Clearly, he hadn't seen the dolls flying at my face. Clearly, he hadn't heard Isabella's voice.

If he had, he wouldn't be acting so calm.

"I know you want to remember your sister," he said. He reached beside me and picked up a photograph on the floor. The same one I'd been holding.

The one I *knew* I had put back. How did it end up on the floor beside me? He looked at it, and a sad smile played across his face. "I know you miss her. Really, I do. But it isn't healthy to dwell."

I wanted to tell him that he had no right to say that, since he'd been shut up in his office ever since she died, but I couldn't bring myself to speak.

"Come on," he said. "We won't tell your mom about this." He held out his hand, and I took it, letting him pull me up to standing. He set the photograph on the dresser when we were upright. Not letting go of my hand, he turned and began walking out of the room, leaving me no choice but to follow.

I looked over my shoulder as we left, staring incredulously at the dolls and the photograph.

The dolls all looked completely normal.

But in the photo, Isabella's eyes glowed red.

15

Dad led me back into my room, which was honestly the last place I wanted to go. The single wall between my bedroom and Isabella's didn't feel like enough. But he knew as well as I did that I needed to clean it, and even though he had a sad, kind expression on his face, I knew he wouldn't let me skip out.

He didn't say anything—the few words we'd exchanged earlier were the most he'd said to me since the funeral. But now that he was here, I didn't want him to go. I didn't want to be alone.

I just couldn't think of anything to say that would make him stay.

"Papa?" I asked as he turned to leave.

"Yes, honey?" He paused in the doorway, looking back at me.

"Do you . . . do you hear her?" I asked. "Do you ever hear her voice?"

It was the closest I could come to asking him if he'd experienced anything strange.

"Of course I do, Maria. I hear her every single day."

Then he left, and I realized two terrible things: one, that he had no idea what was going on, and two, that even after everything, he was still more haunted than I was.

16

Despite everything that had just happened, nothing strange occurred while I was cleaning my room. It was almost unsettling. I put on some music and picked up my clothes and put away a few books and made my bed.

No dolls moved. No photos fell on the floor.

It was almost normal enough to make me think that maybe I'd made everything else up. I mean, it was better than the alternative—that I *had* let something in. That I was being haunted. But I also didn't like the thought that I was losing my grip on reality.

Grief can do funny things, my mom had said the first night I'd woken up from a nightmare. In my dream, Isabella had been alive and happy, and when I woke up, I was so convinced she was alive that I ran into her room and jumped on her bed, only to find it filled with stuffed animals. Mom had come in to find me sobbing amid her pillows. *Sometimes we think we see or hear the people we miss. Like your abuela. Sometimes, when I'm going to sleep, I swear I can hear her singing the same song she hummed when I was your age. When you miss someone, you hold on to a part of them, and they never truly leave you.*

Was that all this was? Grief?

I gathered my dirty clothes and brought them downstairs, still thinking about the possibility that maybe my grief was causing me to think I'd seen or heard strange things. Mom was already making lunch, and some sitcom was playing on the TV, canned laughter dancing around the living room. It was easy to convince myself that everything had only been a hallucination. I just needed sleep. And to eat less sugar before bed tonight.

Most of all, I had to move on.

I unlocked the basement door, flipped on the normal overhead lights, and headed down.

Without the magic of night and the mystery of the twinkle lights, the basement fort looked, well, childish. I paused on the steps, staring at it with mild disappointment in my chest, as if seeing it for the first time. I could remember all the times Isabella and I had played down here—princesses in our castle, sister pirates on a voyage, fellow astronauts on our way to Saturn.

This had been our true home. Our escape from the real world and all its troubles.

Our sanctuary.

When the kids at school made fun of us for being bad at soccer, we could come down here and pretend we were pro athletes hiding from the paparazzi.

When Mom and Dad were fighting—rare, but it happened—we could pretend this was an enchanted forest where only happy kids were allowed.

When it was storming (Isabella was terrified of lightning), this was our cave far beneath the soil, safe from thunder and tornadoes.

The fort was safety. It was where we kept the outside world at bay. Where we lived a better life together.

But in truth, it was just a bunch of pillows and blankets and old holiday lights. There was no magic. It wasn't really a sanctuary. It hadn't kept either of us safe.

Anger suddenly flooded my chest. This place hadn't saved us from anything. It was just one more thing I needed to let go of.

Tomorrow, I told myself. *Tomorrow, I take the fort down and move on.*

I squared my shoulders and descended the last of the steps, heading to the corner where the washer and drier were kept.

When we were younger, we scared ourselves silly coming down here—so much so that there was an entire winter when we refused to even open the basement door.

Mutant spiders scurried in the rafters.

Killer iguanas hid in the laundry machine.

The shadows stretching down the walls were giant bats, waiting for you to turn away so they could wrap their wings around you and suck all your blood.

That particular theory had meant that whenever we came down to grab laundry or some canned food from the shelves, we walked back-to-back, jumping at every shifting shadow and holding our breath.

Without her here, the old fears started to creep in at the edges of my thoughts like mold.

I kept my eyes planted firmly on the washing machine and made my way past the fort, ignoring the shadows and the shifting and the cold that tickled the back of my neck.

I dropped the laundry by the machine and opened the lid to check Dad hadn't left any clothes in there. The barrel was empty, so I grabbed the detergent and fabric softener and poured them in, then hit the button so the machine began to fill with water. Mom told me I should sort my clothes into light and dark, but that seemed like too much work, so I never did. I started dropping my clothes into the water, where they landed with wet splashes.

As I was leaning over to grab the final bunch, I heard it. Through the hiss and gurgle of filling water.

"*Mariaaaa*," the voice whispered. Faint but near. I jerked upright and looked around.

All the lights in the basement were on, and there weren't any shadows to hide in—just the fort, but even that was fully lit and the flaps pulled back, revealing nothing but piles of pillows and rolled sleeping bags.

Was I hearing things?

The goose bumps racing across my arms said I was not.

The desire to race upstairs took hold of my limbs, but I did my best to shake it off. My imagination was just getting the better of me again.

I dropped in the last of the laundry and reached for the lid, but paused.

There was a dress floating on the top of the dirty laundry.

Pale pink.

That wasn't my dress.

That was the dress Isabella had been wearing in the photo.

The dress she had been buried in.

"*Mariaaa . . . ,*" the voice came again.

The water bubbled and churned, even though the machine wasn't moving, even though it was still filling with water. Something swam below the surface, something with black hair and red eyes. A hand reached up from the sodden folds of clothing, a hand with sharp black nails and wrinkled skin, stretching straight toward my face . . .

I didn't wait a second to see what horror would come up from the depths.

I slammed the lid shut and ran upstairs.

Behind me, I swore I heard Isabella laugh.

17

I stood at the top of the basement steps, the door safely closed behind me, and leaned back against the wood frame. Mom was in the living room, which meant she wasn't there to question why I was breathing so quickly, or why tears of fear were pooled in my eyes.

That most definitely was *not* my imagination.

Something had been in the laundry machine. Which meant one undeniable truth: I had released something in this house. And none of us were safe.

I wanted to run into the living room and grab Mom's hand and get her out of the house. But what would I do? What would I say? That we'd been playing with a spirit board in the basement? That I'd been trying to reach Isabella? And maybe I had reached my sister. But I couldn't bring myself to believe that she would appear like this, as some monstrous spirit trying to scare me.

Had I brought back Isabella, or had I also summoned something else?

It didn't matter. I couldn't stay in the house and I couldn't go to Tara's without raising even more suspicion and there was absolutely no way I could tell either of my parents anything.

They wouldn't believe me.

They would think I was trying to get attention.

Worse, I knew that the moment I admitted to trying to talk to Isabella, they would be angry. Mom would believe I had in fact been sneaking into Isabella's room. And then I'd be grounded. Unable to leave.

Trapped in here with a ghost.

It felt like the walls were shrinking in around me. I couldn't breathe. Couldn't focus.

I had to get out.

It felt traitorous. I didn't want to abandon my family. But along with the truth that there was definitely *something* haunting this house came another terrifying reality: It was only targeting me.

I knew Tara would have said something if she'd seen a ghost—she would have yelled at me for inviting it in. Just as I know Lauren would have said something, since a ghost would defy all rational explanation. And my parents . . . they would have freaked out.

The fact that I was the only one seeing this made me feel even more targeted, and even more alone. But at least I could convince myself that if I left, my parents would be safe.

Giggling bubbled up from the basement. Childlike but evil, and most definitely not my sister.

I had to get out of here. *Now.*

I raced to the entryway and grabbed my coat and boots from the closet.

"I'm going for a walk!" I yelled to Mom.

"Is your room clean?"

"Yes! And my clothes are in the wash." *Along*

with a ghost monster that may or may not be con-
nected to Isabella.

But of course I didn't say that. Instead, I slipped on my boots and coat and ran out into the cool afternoon air.

I didn't know where I was going. I just knew I had to walk. Ideally as far away from my haunted house as possible.

My feet automatically started taking me to the elementary school. For a brief second, I considered stopping and taking a detour, but I couldn't think of anywhere else to go, so I followed the impulse.

With every step, the air seemed to grow colder, until—blocks later—I reached the playground.

Even though I'd been here dozens of times since Isabella's death, this was the first time I'd visited after school. The playground was completely empty. There was the new plastic equipment to one side, but I headed over to the older equipment, settling on the swings.

This side of the playground always felt a little sad and abandoned—the rusted slide, the uneven monkey bars, the creaking merry-go-round—which was probably why I felt drawn to it.

I started to swing, and as I got higher, I felt memories bubble to the surface. All the recesses spent laughing and playing games, tag or castles or hide-and-seek. I closed my eyes as tears spilled down my cheeks. All the games we'd never get to play again. All the stories we'd never get to share.

I could practically see us all running around, Tara and Lauren and Isabella and me, yelling and giggling and immersed in our imaginations, playing soccer or just sitting in a circle and talking, carefree, believing we had the whole world ahead of us. Tears flooded out of me, and I squeezed the swing chains tighter as I flew back and forth.

Despite my tears, the memory of our laughter filled my head, until I was positive it was coming from the playground. But I didn't open my eyes. I didn't want to return to reality. I wanted to pretend I could still hear her, that there wasn't a ghost waiting in the halls of my house, that every bad thing that had happened since the summer was just a figment of my imagination. That I hadn't failed the person I loved the most in the world.

With every swing, the air grew colder.

The laughter outside grew louder.

I could hear her. I could *hear* her. If I opened my eyes, I could believe I would see her. But I knew the harsh reality—if I opened my eyes, I would be alone.

So I squeezed my eyes shut tighter and tighter, blacking out the world, trying to drown out everything screaming inside my head.

And then her voice broke over the laughter and the happy screaming.

Isabella's.

"I'm waiting for you, Maria," she said. Her voice was gentle, pleading. *"I've been waiting so long. Come home. Come home and play."*

She sounded like she was right in front of me. It was her. I knew it was her.

I opened my eyes.

And in the moment between darkness and light, I saw her. Floating in front of me. But a moment later, she was gone.

And I realized another stark impossibility:

The playground was dark.

I immediately skidded my feet against the ground, coming to an abrupt halt. My hands trembled against the chains.

"This can't be real."

I blinked multiple times. Waiting for the darkness to clear because it had to just be clouds covering the sun. But moments passed, and it became clear that somehow, in the span of moments, *hours* had passed. I checked my phone on impulse. It was six. Almost dinnertime. How in the world had that happened?

I had no answers. I only knew I didn't want to wait around here anymore. Shadows were stretching from the trees and equipment. Shadows that looked like claws or specters. An icy breeze rustled the trees, making the ghostly shadows claw and grasp. And with it came the sound of giggling. Not just Isabella's—it sounded like dozens of children, all around me, like the playground at recess.

I had thought that leaving the house would make me safer, but clearly that wasn't the case. The last thing I wanted was to blink and have it be mid-night, trapped on a playground and surrounded by ghosts.

Panic racing through my veins and ghosts giggling in my ears, I leaped from the swing and jogged the rest of the way home.

18

At dinner, Mom and I sat at the too-big table together. Dad once more refused to come down. I thought maybe he'd join us since he'd actually spoken to me earlier, but apparently that had been more than enough human interaction for the day. Mom and I poked at the lasagna in silence, classical music playing faintly on the radio. I wasn't hungry at all. After the strange things that had happened today, food was the last thing on my mind.

Especially because nowhere felt safe anymore. Not here, and not outside.

I glanced up at Mom while I ate. She was looking

at her food, distracted, and it was then that I realized she looked older, too. When she wasn't forcing herself to smile or be busy, she had a sort of sadness to her, something deep and immovable, similar to how Dad seemed. There were lines at her eyes, and even though her black hair was shiny and radiant as ever, I could see thicker streaks of white in her ponytail that I didn't think she had a few months ago. She was so sad, but she hid it so well . . .

She looked up, and her smiling mask slid back on, and I quickly looked away, staring instead at the photos Dad had taken that lined our walls.

There were nature shots that he'd been hired to shoot for magazines—the aurora over a snow field that he said was something called a long exposure, a bonfire crackling on the beach while stars glittered overhead, a desert dune under a blazing sun—all large-format and glossy. But the other photos—the most plentiful ones—weren't ones he did for work.

There were photos of him and Mom on their wedding, her in lacy white and looking happier than ever, him in a sharp tux with a ridiculously large flower pinned to the front. Photos of their vacations to tropical beaches or camping in the wild. And even more numerous were the photos of us. Isabella and Mom and me—sometimes with Dad in the frame, but usually without since he would often take the photos and forget his tripod at home—at parks or museums or in front of the school building. There were photos of Isabella blowing out her birthday candles, shots of me and her dressed as queens in regal robes that were actually bedsheets we stole, pictures of us as babies or toddlers or little kids.

We were everywhere.

And I thought, *Maybe that was why Dad didn't like eating down here.*

There were too many reminders of what he'd lost.

I swallowed hard.

Would he keep taking photos?

Would there be pictures up there someday of just me? Me in front of the school when it should be me and Isabella. Me graduating. Me getting a car or moving out or . . .

Me growing up.

Alone.

Suddenly, even though Mom was still in the room, I felt terribly alone, as if the future was one long, bleak hallway that I couldn't stop walking down.

Isabella, I wish—

A cold hand clamped down on my shoulder.

I yelped and jerked, but there was no one there.

"Are you okay, honey?" Mom asked. She looked concerned, but even that was another mask. If she was taking care of me, she didn't have time to be sad.

"Just cold," I said, shivering dramatically.

The shiver wasn't entirely an act.

I could still feel the cold handprint on my shoulder, and it seemed to drip under my skin and down my spine like trickling ice water.

She chuckled. "So melodramatic. But I'll turn the heat up for you."

She stood and went into the living room to turn up the thermostat.

The moment she was gone, the temperature

seemed to drop thirty degrees, as if I'd just fallen into the Arctic Circle.

My next exhale came out in a cloud.

"Are you there?" I whispered, watching my breath dance in a white puff before me.

My breath cleared, and I looked down at my water glass.

The fogged water glass.

On it were two words, dripping condensation like blood.

YOUR FAULT

19

I lay back in bed, staring at the shadows and streaks of light on my wall made by the streetlamps and passing cars outside. My stuffed animals lay scattered at the foot of my bed—all except the rabbit, which I'd stuffed inside the top drawer of my dresser, because I knew for certain that it had moved earlier.

All I could hear was the faint rumble of the television downstairs and the drone of passing cars outside. I didn't want to close my eyes. I didn't want to sleep.

I felt very, very alone. But also like the shadows were watching me.

Ages ago, Isabella and I would knock quietly on the wall behind our headboards—the wall connecting our two rooms—and we made a sort of Morse code. Three knocks meant *Are you awake?* and one knock meant yes, two meant no. (Obviously, no response also meant no, but since Isabella almost always knocked harder than she needed to, I was awake no matter what. I pretty much always knocked two times, just to tease her.)

A part of me wanted to knock on the wall. Just because. But I didn't.

The truth was, I didn't want to hear an answer.

I tried to stay awake. But I hadn't slept much last night, and the fear of everything that had happened today had drained me, like I'd gone on one long run. No matter how hard I tried to fight it off, sleep fell heavily around me.

And as I felt myself drift, I heard on the wall behind me three quiet knocks.

20

I woke with a start.

I'd been dreaming about . . . actually, I didn't know what I'd been dreaming about, but it couldn't have been good, nor could it have been for very long. It was still dark out, and even though I couldn't hear the TV going downstairs, it didn't feel like I'd been asleep for more than ten minutes.

My heart hammered in my chest.

Something had woken me up. But what?

My room was silent. The slashes of light on the wall were still.

I sat up a little taller in bed, looking around, wondering if maybe I'd heard a noise outside—

A shadow scurried across the floor to my book bag, darker than all the rest.

I jerked my head toward the movement.

It looked like it had come from my dresser . . .

My dresser!

A streetlight illuminated the surface. There were the photos of Isabella and me. The trophies and ribbons from school. And the top drawer was open.

Something giggled from behind my book bag.

A shadow darted out from behind it, this time going straight to the closet.

The closet door screeched and swayed slightly from the movement.

I couldn't breathe. Fear had lodged my breath in my throat. I couldn't scream if I wanted to.

And I wanted to.

Something

was moving

in my room!

At first I thought it was a rat. A big, furry rat with
a gross snakelike tail and big teeth and—
                    giggling echoed from my closet. Isabella's
                    voice. But darker. Sinister. I watched
                    in horror as the door slowly opened
                    and the shadow crept out. Inch by inch
                    along the wall.
As if it knew I was watching,
        as if it wanted to drag out my terror.
And then it began
        moving
                            up.
Straight up the wall, a dark smear in the shadows.
It passed through a streak of streetlight.
                    Not a rat.
Not any living thing.
        It was my stuffed rabbit.
Scurrying up the wall like a spider.
        Scuttling across the ceiling.
                        Until it was right
                        over
                                me.

I looked up in horror as the stuffed rabbit paused impossibly, right above my bed, right above my pillow.

I saw its head move, its ears flop, as it tilted to look straight at me. Two pinpricks of red began to glow in the darkness, its burning eyes stabbing into my soul.

"You let me in," it giggled with Isabella's voice. "Now I'm never going to leave. And neither will **YOU!**"

Its mouth opened wide, yawning with a darkness deeper than the blackest night.

And before I could scream, before I could think to jerk away, it dropped from the ceiling and swallowed me whole.

21

When I opened my eyes again, I couldn't tell if I was dreaming or wide-awake. I couldn't trust my senses to be sure.

Sunlight streamed through the windows, and birds sang outside. And the top drawer of my dresser was still firmly shut, the rabbit nowhere to be seen.

"Was it just a bad dream?" I whispered to myself, looking around. My other stuffed animals were scattered on the floor, but that was probably just from me tossing and turning all night.

Shakily, I stood and went over to the dresser.

My fingers trembled as I pulled out the stuffed rabbit and turned it this way and that.

It didn't look any different. It didn't *look* like it could walk up the walls. Especially in the light of day with the chirping birds and the smell of coffee drifting up from downstairs. It was a perfect, sunny Sunday morning. It felt like nothing bad could happen on a day like today. Nothing strange.

That's what you thought the day Isabella died, too.

I set down the rabbit and forced away the thought, making my way to the kitchen for breakfast before I could get too sad.

Surprisingly, my dad was down at the table, eating cereal and talking quietly to Mom. They both looked up when I entered.

"Hey, sunshine," he said. His voice was tired.

"Morning, Dad," I replied.

Mom poured me some cereal, and I sat down next to him.

"Your mother and I were thinking of taking a little day trip," he said. "Just the two of us. Would you be okay staying here on your own? We'd be back by dinner. You're welcome to have your friends over if you like."

No.

Don't leave me alone in here, not even for a second. You don't know what's in these walls.

But of course I didn't say that. I couldn't. Not only because I couldn't explain it, but because I could tell from the look in his eyes that he was really hoping I'd say yes. They needed this. In the back of my mind, I heard Isabella cackle: *I'm never going to leave, and neither will you!*

I knew I couldn't refuse, though. Dad looked so tired, and so sad, and I had a feeling that going for a drive with Mom might be the one thing that would cheer him up. Maybe he would even take some photos. They used to go on drives all the time before Isabella died. There were some really nice hiking trails outside our town, and they said it helped them reconnect. I was surprised they didn't insist on hiring a babysitter. Either they really trusted me, or they really needed to get out of the house.

"Okay," I said reluctantly. "Sure. I bet Tara could come over."

"Thanks, honey," Mom said. "Are you sure you'll be okay?"

"Yeah. Positive."

I wasn't. And I knew, the moment the words had left my lips, that I was doomed.

22

My parents left for their drive just after breakfast. Sure enough, Dad brought along some of his photo equipment; the sight of him dragging out his gear gave me a strange sense of hope. Maybe things *could* go back to normal. Maybe the nightmare was about to end.

The moment they left, though, those hopeful thoughts vanished as the weight of the house settled over me. As the presence of whatever I'd invited in made itself known. I could feel eyes on the back of my neck. The temperature of the house seemed to drop as my parents drove off. I watched them from the window, part of me wanting to run outside and the other knowing that that wouldn't actually help.

It was clear I couldn't run from this. Whatever it was. I needed to face it. And that meant I needed to know who—or what—I was facing.

I'd already called Tara to see if she could come over, and she said she would in a few hours. Which gave me time to figure this out.

I didn't have the spirit board, but I did have creativity.

Reluctantly turning from the window, I went over to the closet and grabbed some paper and pens. Minutes later, I'd written the full alphabet over the paper, as well as *YES* and *NO*, just like the spirit board. Only in purple pen. I didn't have a pointer, so I just picked a bottle cap from the recycling and put it on the board. My fingertips barely fit on it.

I hesitated.

Did I really want to do this?

What's the worst that could happen? an unhelpful voice asked. *You've already invited it in.*

I swallowed, fear and shame warring within me.

"Okay," I whispered. I closed my eyes and tried to calm my mind. "I call out to whatever spirit is in my house. Are you there?"

For a moment, nothing happened. What if it didn't work with only one person? I mean, it did before, but Tara had been there at the start. What if it wouldn't work without the real board?

Just then, the cap twitched, nearly shooting out from under my fingers.

YES

Even though I had hoped for this sort of reaction, I still jolted back in my chair.

"Who . . . who are you?" I whispered. I reached my trembling hands forward, but the cap started moving before I could touch it.

Y
O
U
R
S
I
S

T
E
R

"Isabella?"

Hope and fear warred in my chest.

If this *was* Isabella, why was she being so mean? Why was she trying to scare me?

The moment I thought it, the cap started moving again, and with every letter, my blood chilled another degree.

Y
O
U

K
I
L
L

E
D

M
E

"No," I whispered in shock, my hands clutching my frantic heart. "I wouldn't have—I never—"

Y
O
U
R
F
A
U
L
T

"No," I said. I pushed the chair back and stood up. "No, that's not true. You know that's not true. I didn't want—"

But the cap kept moving, and my words faltered.

Y
O
U
R
E
N

E
X
T

The cap flew off the board, smashing into a glass by the sink and making it shatter. I yelped in fear as the handmade board burst into flame, immediately turning to ash.

And from upstairs came a deafening *BOOM*.

23

No. No, no, no, no, *no.*

I was *not* going to stay here any longer.

Making sure to avoid the broken glass, I ran out of the kitchen and toward the front door. The moment my hand touched the knob, however, I heard a voice.

Isabella's voice.

"Help me, Maria," she pleaded. *"Please. Help me!"*

And it was coming from upstairs.

I swallowed hard, fear raging against doubt. What

if it was really her? What if she really needed me?

What if . . . what if her soul was trapped here by some evil spirit? That might explain the strange messages. Unless it was just an evil spirit messing with me and she was nowhere to be seen. But was I willing to take that chance?

If I left and she actually needed help, I'd be failing her.

Again.

"Okay," I said, maybe to her and maybe to myself. "Okay. I'll help you."

I turned from the door and headed toward the stairs.

The air grew colder with every echoing step. At the very top, my breath came out in clouds. Maybe I should turn around? Maybe this was a mistake? But it was too late to turn around. If my sister needed me, I would help. I had to take that risk.

I reached the top step.

"Isabella?" I whispered, peering around the corner. "Are you there?"

A shadow darted from my room to Isabella's.

SLAM!

Isabella's door slammed shut, shaking the walls, sending a photo crashing to the floor. I shrieked and froze, my feet stuck to the stair like glue. I couldn't move if I wanted to.

And I wanted to.

I could only stare at the photo—it was the one of me and Isabella at soccer practice, our knees dirty and our smiles wide. My breath was solid, heavy as concrete in my lungs. I couldn't breathe. Couldn't move.

"Isabella?"

Slowly—

> ever
>
> so
>
> slowly
>
>> —Isabella's door opened.

Just a little bit.

Just enough for me to see two red eyes peering out from the shadows.

Before I could see the monster waiting behind the door, my feet finally became unglued as fear turned to panic.

I turned and fled down the stairs.

24

I thundered down the steps, nearly tripping over my own feet in my haste to get as far away from the nightmare as possible.

And when I saw the shadow waiting outside the front door, I stumbled and caught myself from falling just in time, a scream stifled in the back of my throat.

But then the shadow . . . knocked?

I blinked and realized it was just Tara behind the door.

Quickly, I pulled open the door, fully intending to grab her by the arm and drag her as far away from my house as possible.

I didn't get the chance.

The moment the door opened, Tara rushed in, panic clear on her face.

"What happened? Are you okay?" she asked, quickly scanning the room.

Her reaction caught me off guard.

"What—what are you talking about?" I asked. *What are you doing here already? There's no way you finished your chores that fast!*

"Your text!" she said.

"My . . . text?"

"Yeah, Maria, your text!" Her eyebrows furrowed, but she grabbed her phone from her pocket and held it up to me, showing me our latest text exchange.

The last thing I sent to her *should* have been: **great, cya after chores.**

Instead, it read: **Help! I think I broke my ankle and I'm home alone!**

I definitely did *not* send that last text.

Which Tara was definitely starting to grasp, judging from the way she was looking at my feet.

"Was this some sort of joke?" she asked. "I thought you were hurt! I ran right over!"

"N-no," I stuttered, my brain spinning quickly but getting nowhere. I hadn't sent that text. I hadn't even touched my phone since we last texted. It was up in my room . . .

My room! The shadow had been in my room!

I looked up the stairs, the hairs on the back of my neck standing on end as a terrible thought raced through me.

What if the shadow had sent the message?

What if it wanted Tara here with me?

Why? Whatever it was, it couldn't be good.

"We have to go," I said. I grabbed Tara's arm. I'd explain later. Or I'd *try* to explain later.

"Maria, what—"

A creak upstairs cut her off.

The creak of an opening door.

I knew it was Isabella's door.

And before I could take Tara and flee, Isabella's cruel laughter drifted down the stairs.

25

"Maria," Tara whispered. She trembled at my side, stepping in closer, her voice quivering. "Please tell me this is a prank."

I couldn't answer. Couldn't move. I could only watch as shadows pooled at the top of the staircase and dripped down the steps—Tara clenched my arm so tightly it hurt.

The giggling from the shadows turned to speech, a voice just like Isabella's, but colder, more cruel. The voice that had haunted my dreams.

"I'm heee-rrrre," the voice said. *"You let me in. You wanted to play. And now we're never going to leave!"*

Just like that, the front door slammed shut, the dead bolt sliding into place. All around the house, I heard doors and windows slam. The loud noises spurred me to action. I turned and grabbed the handle, but the lock wouldn't budge, and a second later, I yelped and leaped back as a jolt of electricity shot through my hands.

Tara stood there, frozen, staring at the heavy darkness at the top of the stairs. It was starting to congeal, thick like tar, bubbling and forming into the shape of a child. A girl. But I couldn't convince myself it looked like Isabella. It sort of did, but even in outline, the figure looked, somehow, cruel. And then the shadow blinked, revealing two crimson eyes.

"Maria . . . Is that . . . is that . . . ?"

"I don't know," I said. I reached out and took Tara's hand. "We have to get out of here. Come on!"

Thankfully, she didn't fight back—she broke from her stupor immediately and followed as I led her into the kitchen, trying the back door. But it, too, was locked, and I removed my hand quickly before I could get another jolt of static. Tara was at the window, trying to pry it open, but it wouldn't budge.

"It's no use!" she called, panic clear in her voice. "They're all locked! We're trapped."

I glanced around. Footsteps echoed upstairs, right above our heads, a thunder that echoed inside my bones. I caught sight of the basement door, the warm, shimmering glow of twinkle lights. My sanctuary. I don't know why, but I started walking toward it.

"Come on," I said. "We can hide down here."

"Hide? From a ghost?"

26

Before the words even left her lips, I knew it was a bad idea.

Going into the basement with no exit was clearly not the safe bet. But there was nowhere else to go—we couldn't leave, and we surely weren't going upstairs. The basement was the only place left. Plus . . . it was Isabella's and my safe place. It was where we could escape from the real world, and maybe that meant I could escape the spirit plaguing us.

We stumbled quickly down the steps, heading straight toward the blanket fort, where warm lights glittered invitingly. I pulled back the entrance curtain and jumped inside, Tara right beside me. Together, we buried ourselves under the piles of blankets and sleeping bags and pillows and tried to steady our breathing.

Tried to become as silent as possible.

Tried to pretend that nothing—not the ghost, not even us—was there.

Silence fell around us, our ragged breathing muffled by the blankets. I could feel Tara shivering beside me. I wanted to say a dozen things—to apologize that she was here, to ask what she thought was going on, to try and convince her that we would surely find a way out of this.

Even though I wasn't certain of that myself.

The worst part was, I knew the spirit was right—this was my fault. Not just Isabella's death, but the haunting. I had invited it in. Which meant I had put everyone I loved in danger. Again.

Silence stretched.

Seconds crept by, slow as minutes. Sweat gathered on my forehead, and I wanted nothing more than to rip off the blankets and make a run for it.

Not that I thought I could run anywhere. The playground had already proven as much.

> *CREAK.*

The basement door slowly opened, the sound somehow sharp even through the layers of blankets.

I heard Tara inhale in fear.

I held my breath.

> *THUD.*

> A footstep, creaking on the wooden planks.

> *THUD.*

> Another, getting nearer.

THUD.

> I reached as quietly as I could under the blankets and took Tara's trembling hand.

THUD.

> "*Come out, come out, wherever you are,*" came Isabella's cold, cruel voice.

27

THUD.

There were only five steps. Which meant she had reached the bottom.

Silence fell once more. She could be anywhere.

Anywhere.

Despite the layers of blankets, I felt my skin grow cold.

Fabric rustled as the entry was swept aside.

"Don't hide from me, dear sister," Isabella cooed. "I've waited so long to play with you."

It felt like my heart was ripping in two. I wanted so badly to believe that it was my sister. Wanted to think that she was here, and she'd missed me, and forgave me. But I couldn't shake the terror of those burning red eyes, the violence of the shattering glass in the kitchen. The blankets by my toes shifted as a ghostly footstep crept closer. A part of me wanted to pull back the covers, to hug the girl I longed to see so badly.

But it wasn't her. It couldn't be.

I knew Isabella better than anyone else. And I knew she would never be this cruel.

I squeezed my eyes shut and hoped the monster would go away.

"Oh, did you want to play a game?" Isabella asked. "Hide-and-seek?" She chuckled, her voice sending more chills down my spine as her voice took on a menacing tone.

Slowly—

ever

so

slowly

—someone peeled back the blankets from my face.

I bit my lip to keep from crying out in fear, so hard I tasted blood.

Lights burst behind my closed eyelids as the covers fell away.

I bit down a moan of dread.

I wouldn't open my eyes.

I didn't want to see it.

Her.

Because I knew it wouldn't be Isabella, but I wanted so badly for it to be.

Cold breath tickled the back of my neck. I could hear the ghost *breathe*. I squeezed my eyes even tighter and tried not to cry.

"I found you, Maria," the ghost said, her voice cracking, becoming even less like the one that I missed. "But I'll let you try again. A second chance. Like the one I never received."

I felt her lean in, felt the coldness of her skin, smelled the trace of her shampoo. Isabella's shampoo. But this time, it smelled faintly of dirt and decay. When she spoke again, my nostrils filled with the scent of rot.

"Just remember, this is your fault. All of it. You're the reason I'm dead. And soon, you both will join me. But first, we're going to have some fun."

She cackled.

The basement lights flickered.

Silence settled around us. The world became warm again. And when I thought it was safe, I finally opened my eyes.

She was gone.

But the nightmare, I knew, was not.

28

I glanced around the fort, but it was empty, save the trembling pile of blankets beside me that hid Tara.

I sat there for a few moments, staring at shadows, waiting for the spirit or whatever it was to come back. Nothing moved. No shifting shadows, no creaking steps. Just silence and the muffled sounds of Tara's terrified breathing.

"She's gone," I whispered, disbelief tinging my voice. "It's okay, you can come out."

Tara hesitantly poked her head out of the covers, her hair all mussed and frizzy. When she saw the coast was clear, she shoved all the blankets aside and stared at me.

"What in the *world* is going on?" she hissed, her words coming out in an avalanche. "What was that, Maria? Was that a ghost? Was that Isabella? And what did it mean that this was all your fault?" Her eyes widened. "Wait. You didn't. You told me you didn't!"

I looked away as she realized the truth.

"Maria!" she yelped. "I *told* you not to invite it in. I *told* you!"

The lights shimmered, but not from any ghostly entity—from the tears that started to cloud my vision as I fought down my anger. The anger and frustration I felt toward myself. And at the rest of the world for what it did to me.

"You don't understand," I whispered. "You don't know what it's like."

"I've been trying," Tara said. "Ever since . . ." She took a deep breath. "Ever since Isabella died, I've tried to—"

"You don't get it," I interrupted, finally looking at her. "It's like a part of me is missing. There's nothing anyone can do to fill her place. To undo what happened. I would do anything to get her back. Anything!"

"Including inviting an evil spirit into your home?" Tara asked quietly.

"You don't know that's what it is," I whispered, my anger fading immediately, replaced quickly with doubt and guilt.

Tara raised an eyebrow. "Then what else could it be? You invited the spirit we were talking to into your home. You heard it! Now we're never getting out of here."

"She said she was Isabella." My voice faltered. Even *I* knew that wasn't true.

"It lied," Tara said. "Whatever it is, that's *not* Isabella and you know it. Isabella wasn't cruel. She would never do this to us."

I knew two things for certain the moment she said it.

One, that she was right—Isabella had her

moments, but she was never this mean. She would never have sought revenge. Not even after what had happened. Not even when it had been my fault.

And two, whatever it was that I'd unleashed was only just beginning to torment us, and it wouldn't stop until we died of fright.

29

We didn't dare move from the fort.

For a long while, we just sat there, cowering in the blankets, watching the shadows warily. It was silly to think that we were safe here. But the seconds passed, and the basement was quiet and empty, and it was easy—far too easy—to want to convince myself that the terror was over. That the ghost was gone.

But I knew it wasn't gone.

I knew it was waiting for us to move so it could scare us again.

"Maria," Tara whispered, "what did it mean

about this being your fault? Why did it say that you're the reason Isabella is dead?"

Her voice squeaked. I looked down, my breath suddenly as panicked as when the ghost had been near.

Could I tell her? Could I tell her the horrible truth? I stalled, fiddling with the blanket.

Suddenly, Tara gasped, and I nearly leaped out of my skin thinking she'd seen something. But her eyes were wide not with fear, but excitement.

"I know what to do!" she whispered wildly. "We can call our parents! They'll come get us."

"But my phone is in my room," I whispered back. And she knew we didn't have a landline.

"But mine's right here," she replied. She fished into her pocket and pulled out her cell phone. As she looked at it and tapped the buttons, however, her face fell. "It's dead. How is it already dead?"

As one, we both glanced up, looking for the spirit that had drained her battery as sure as it had trapped us in the house. It had gotten rid of any chance we had at escaping.

"Maybe we could just wait down here? My parents should be back soon. We can wait until they're home and then they could help."

"But that could take *hours*," Tara whimpered.

The thought had crossed my mind, too, and before I could suggest again that maybe staying down here would be relatively safe, there was a soft *thump*.

From the corner of the basement.

From the place all our Halloween decorations were stored.

Tara and I stared at each other, wide-eyed with fear, as more noises filled the basement.

The rip of cardboard.

The creak of plastic joints.

The chittering laughter of bats.

"It's time to play!" Isabella's terrifying voice laughed.

And then, before we could even think of running, the flap of the fort ripped open and the monsters flooded in.

30

I screamed in terror as all the Halloween decorations we stored in the basement appeared in the fort's entrance.

Instantly, the fort was filled with plastic bats that flapped and swirled around us, tangling in our hair and dive-bombing into our blankets. On impulse, we grabbed for a blanket and hid under it, but the safety was short-lived. A second later, the fabric was ripped out of our fingers by the plastic skeletons that crawled along the floor. Their broken jaws cackled as they made their way toward us, scrabbling over the stolen blanket. More skeletons scratched against the fort walls, trying to break in.

"Run!" I screamed.

We pushed backward, toward an opening, Tara in the lead. The moment she was free, she yelped in fear and stumbled.

She had run straight into a fake cobweb.

It wrapped around her, cocooning her in thick white webbing. I dropped to my knees and began ripping the web off her, but it had a mind of its own. And as I peeled away the thick tufts, small black spiders began to swarm toward us, their little plastic legs clacking on the floor. Tara saw them and began to scream.

I pulled faster, yanking a great patch off her in the nick of time. She busted her way through and scrambled to her feet, just as the spiders neared.

A second slower, and she would have been engulfed.

"Go!" she yelled, racing toward the stairs. The skeletons and spiders followed, snapping at our heels. Something shifted ahead of us, and for a moment, I thought it was rocks rolling along the ground. Then I saw the flash of lights and realized it was the plastic jack-o'-lanterns we'd stored down here. They rolled toward us, trying to trip us up, their creepy smiles glowing brightly and cackles echoing from their hollow mouths.

We jumped over them, trying not to trip, and raced to the basement steps.

I screamed as a great ghoul—the very one I'd bought with my allowance money last year—billowed up from beneath the stairs, cackling and laughing, her eyes glowing green and her hands out-stretched in bony claws.

"You'll never escape!" she howled with mad glee. "You've let me in, and now we will play, forever!"

The ghoul swooped toward us and I yelled out in fright, but Tara acted quickly. She grabbed a ten-nis racket that had been leaning against the wall and swatted at the demonic decoration. It flew to the side of the basement and crashed into the boxes, sending a cascade of cardboard to the floor.

"Nice one!" I yelled.

She nodded, a grim smile on her face, and—still clutching the racket—we stormed up to the main floor, bursting out of the shadowy basement and into the warm sunlight.

I slammed the door shut behind us and leaned against it. My breath was hot and fast in my throat, and I looked around the kitchen on high alert, ready for whatever new terror the spirit would throw at us.

Birds chirped outside the window. The fridge hummed quietly. Beyond that, nothing moved or made a sound beside Tara's and my frantic breathing.

Even the decorations in the basement had gone silent.

A small, small part of me wanted to open the door and peek back down, to see if they were still possessed.

The rest of me said that was a terrible idea.

"What do we do?" Tara asked.

She watched as I moved away from the basement door and went over to the kitchen window, trying to budge it open. It was still locked tight. Outside, the day went on unawares. I pounded on the glass frame, but it didn't shatter, and the neighbor walking her dog didn't notice, no matter how hard I pounded. I moved to the kitchen door, but it, too, was still latched tight, the doorknob buzzing with dangerous static.

"I don't know," I said. I went back to the window and pounded on it once more. The frame rattled, but nothing gave. "We can't get out and the phones are dead. Maybe . . . maybe we can flag someone down. It's the middle of the afternoon. I bet we can stop someone walking outside."

She nodded. But before we could leave the kitchen, a terrible laughter froze me in my tracks.

As did the array of forks and knives that burst from the kitchen drawer and hovered in midair, all pointed directly at me.

31

Tara yelped and pressed herself hard against the basement door.

"No one will help you," came not-Isabella's dark voice. It seemed to come from everywhere and nowhere, as if the very house breathed her words. "Why should they, when you didn't help me? I bet you won't even help your best friend."

"Maria," Tara said, her voice trembling as she stared at the cutlery pointing at my chest. "What is she talking about?"

"She doesn't know?" Isabella asked. The cutlery

quivered. "She doesn't know the real reason your sister died?"

Tara took a step forward, and a butter knife flipped over in midair, pointing at her. She stopped in her tracks.

"Isabella died because Maria abandoned her," Isabella's cruel voice hissed. "But don't worry, Tara. You'll know how that feels soon enough. Let's see if Maria cares enough about *you* to try and save you!"

Before either of us could ask what in the world the ghost meant, the basement door burst open and the horde of nightmare decorations spilled out. Skeletons grabbed Tara's ankles and ghouls clasped her arms and spiderwebs wrapped around her mouth in a gag. Her eyes widened, her muffled screams cutting through the kitchen.

Then the decorations dragged her back into the basement.

The door clicked shut behind her.

The cutlery floating before me clattered to the floor.

I ran forward and banged on the basement door. The doorknob wouldn't budge—it was locked tight.

"Tara!" I yelled. "Tara! Are you okay?"

I held my breath and pressed my ear to the door.

Silence. No screams or thuds from the basement. No cackles of ghostly triumph. Just silence.

I pounded on the door again, tried the handle one more time. But it didn't budge. Tara didn't call back.

I had failed to save her. Just like I'd failed Isabella.

32

I pressed my forehead against the door. Tears spilled down my cheeks and dripped to my feet.

"I'm sorry," I whispered. "I'm so, so sorry."

I didn't know if I was talking to Tara or to Isabella.

I pounded on the door a third time.

And this time, I heard a click. The door unlocked. I stepped back, uncertain, and gently tested the doorknob. It wasn't electrified. Could it be?

I yanked the door open and looked down the basement steps.

Light flickered from the fairy lights, casting soft

shadows over the blanket fort and the pillows scattered about. Everything was neat and orderly, just as it had been this morning, before the chaos began.

No decorations tumbled from their boxes.

No tangled blankets.

"Tara!" I yelled out.

The entrance to the fort was open, revealing a completely empty interior. And even though there were shadows lurking in the corners of the basement, I knew that Tara wasn't there.

I ran down the steps. The tennis racket she'd grabbed was at the bottom, and I picked it up, ready to defend myself. But nothing stirred in the basement. My heart hammering, I ran over to the blanket fort and pulled all the sheets down and poked through the sleeping bags and pillows.

She wasn't there.

I ran over to the corner shelf, to where the Halloween decorations had been. Using the tennis racket to pop off a lid, I glanced inside—all the decorations were put neatly away, just as Mom had done almost a year ago, as if they hadn't moved.

Where had they taken her? What was going on? Had she just vanished?

"Where are you?" I whispered.

As if in answer, something rustled behind me.

33

I turned, and there was my stuffed rabbit, perched at the top of the basement steps, light from the kitchen turning it into a black silhouette with ruby-red eyes.

"I hope you aren't giving up just yet," Isabella's voice growled from the rabbit's mouth. "I was just starting to have fun."

"This isn't a game!" I yelled out, my voice quivering with unshed tears. "Give her back!"

Something shifted behind the rabbit. A shadow-like fog, a mirage in the light. In the shape of a girl.

"Now, why would I do that?" Isabella asked. "This *is* a game, Maria. After all, when you invited me in, you thought it was a game, didn't you? I'm just continuing the fun. And I think we should play hide-and-seek."

"I'm not going to play your games," I replied. I didn't know where the words came from—I certainly wasn't feeling brave. In fact, I felt horribly, horribly afraid.

"Oh, but you will. If you ever hope to save Tara. Or are you going to turn away and pretend this isn't your fault? Just like you did with me?"

The rabbit's eyes glowed brighter, and the shadowlike form behind it grew more solid, became the blur of a girl. And she looked an awful lot like Isabella.

"You're not my sister," I replied. "She would never do this to me. She would never want to hurt or scare me."

Instantly, the fog at the top of the steps vanished, then reappeared right in front of me. More solid. Like a wavering reflection.

It was Isabella.

Isabella, right before she'd been hit by the car.

In the same dress. The same angry eyes.

"You wanted me gone," she growled. "And you got your wish. You say I would never hurt or scare you, but look what you did to me! Why should I not do the same to you?"

I took a step back.

"I'm sorry," I whispered. Tears brimmed in my eyes.

"Sorry doesn't change anything," Isabella said. She tilted her head to the side, and that's when I saw it.

A flicker in her face.

Just for an instant, she looked like someone else. Someone older. A woman with cracked skin and fierce eyes and tangled hair. Then I blinked, and it was Isabella once more. She smiled, her lips going so wide I could see her blackened gums.

"So we will play a game," she said. "Because you said you missed me. We will play, and if you find your friend, I will let you live. Both of you. But if not . . ." Her smile widened with the threat. Her face cracked. I could almost see the terrifying old woman behind the mask of Isabella. Almost.

She leaned in. Even though she was a ghost, I could smell Isabella's shampoo. Mixed with the unmistakable scent of graveyard dirt.

"Save Tara, but think about this—if you save her, you're only proving that you care about her more than you ever cared about your sister. You're proving that you wanted Isabella gone. We both know you could have saved her, but you didn't. You didn't care at all. So what would you rather prove yourself to be? A terrible friend or a terrible sister?"

She stood up. Her smile dropped.

"Begin."

In a whirl of shadow, Isabella vanished.

34

Shame and sadness flooded me. I dropped my head into my hands and started to cry.

The ghost was right.

It didn't matter if it was Isabella or not—she was right.

All the cruel things I'd thought to myself, she'd said aloud and confirmed.

I *could* have saved my sister.

I *could* have tried harder.

If only I'd called out.

The memory tried to scratch its way to the surface, but I pushed it down. I wouldn't let it overtake me. Not now. Not ever. I couldn't look at what I'd done. Not unless I wanted to fall apart entirely.

I hadn't saved Isabella. But I was going to save Tara no matter what. She didn't deserve to be trapped in here with me. None of this was her fault. And I wasn't going to let Isabella's spirit take out her vengeance on my friend.

Only . . . was it truly Isabella?

I kept remembering the way she looked. Yes, at times she looked like my sister. But there were moments when her face or voice cracked, and she sounded altogether different. Older. Angrier. I didn't want to believe it was truly my sister. So how did she know all my secrets?

I shook my head. There was time to worry about that later. First, I had to find Tara.

The basement door was still open, letting in the warm afternoon sunlight, but the rabbit and the ghost of Isabella were both gone.

The kitchen was equally empty. What was even stranger—the cutlery that had held me captive only minutes before was gone from the floor. I went over and pulled open the drawer just to make sure the forks and knives weren't floating somewhere else in the house. But there they were, put neatly away.

Just like the Halloween decorations.

The entire house was silent. So quiet I could hear the blood pounding in my ears. Slowly, I made my way into the dining room, and then the living room. No sign of Isabella's ghost or Tara. I even poked open the entryway closet, but she wasn't in there either.

I didn't expect the ghost to make it that easy.

I made my way to the foot of the stairs and looked up.

Shadows hung heavy in the hall above, as if the entire hallway had been bathed in darkness. When I exhaled, my breath came out in a cloud.

A darker shadow scurried across the hall, just visible from the bottom of the steps. A squat shadow with bright red eyes.

The rabbit.

Watching me.

Undoubtedly off to tell Isabella I was near.

Chills raced across my arms at the thought. But I had to face this. I had to find Tara.

"I'm coming for you," I whispered, and slowly, steadily, made my way up the stairs.

It was time to face the monster I had made.

35

I told myself I was shivering because of the cold that wrapped around my limbs the moment I reached the upstairs hall. But that wasn't the whole truth.

I was shivering because I was scared.

The hallway was not what I remembered. Not as it should be.

The photos along the walls—most of them photos of Isabella and me—were all still there. But something was different, and I had to look closer to find out what. In most of the photos, Isabella and I were facing away from the camera, so only the backs of our heads could be seen. In others, my face had been scratched out, with horrible words like *LIAR* and *KILLER* written in marker over them. Each made my heart sink. Because I knew they were the truth. Shadows curled in the corners of the ceiling like snakes, curtaining the whole hallway in frigid darkness.

Both my parents' door and Isabella's door were closed. Mine was cracked open.

"Tara?" I whispered, not daring to raise my voice any further. "Tara, where are you?"

Someone mumbled at the far end of the hall.

In my room.

I couldn't be sure, but it sounded a lot like Tara.

I swallowed my fear and gripped the racket tighter, then made my way into my bedroom.

Carefully, I peeked through the crack in the door and looked inside my room. It was exactly as I had left it. The bed neatly made, my stuffed animals and dolls neatly arranged, my books all in order. I opened the door wider and stepped inside.

Exactly as I had left it, and the stuffed rabbit was nowhere to be seen.

I looked down at my feet on instinct, then up to the ceiling above my bed. Nothing.

"Tara?" I whispered again. I looked around, but there were really only two places she could be hiding—in my closet, or under the bed.

I didn't want to check either of those places.

Even though it was the middle of the day, I flipped on the light switch to the room. The lights made a strange buzzing noise, but didn't turn on. *Great*.

"Tara?"

Nothing.

I took a hesitant step into the room, and the door clicked shut behind me.

36

I didn't check to see if the door had locked. It was too late now. Trembling, I dropped to my knees and used the tennis racket to lift the corner of my bedspread.

The sight of boxes and shoes and a couple of books greeted me, and I let out a sigh of relief I hadn't realized I was holding in.

Nothing dangerous or scary under here.

Another muffled noise, and I was certain it was coming from the closet. I dropped the comforter and began to stand up—

—and found myself staring into the beady eyes of all my dolls.

I screamed and stumbled backward, dropping the racket in my haste. The bedroom door pressed against my back as I crouched there, shaking, staring at the row of dolls that had impossibly lined up on the edge of my bed.

Every.

Single.

Eye.

Was trained on me.

"What's the matter?" the dolls said in unison, their voices high-pitched and scratchy. Their eyes began to glow red. **"Don't you want to play with us?"** I watched, frozen, as they slowly lifted off the bed, hovering in midair. **"Because we want to play with you. We all want to play."**

On cue, every single toy in my room began to hover. The stuffed animals lifted from my bed, circling above my head, and the books on my shelf fell out and began flapping around like birds, shedding ripped pages all over the floor. The sound of ripping and shredding mingled with the demonic laughter that seemed to come from everywhere all at once.

"Get away," I said, my words trembling. "Get out of my house. You aren't welcome here."

"But, Maria . . . ," the voices replied. They began to meld together. Began to sound like Isabella once more. "This is our home. It has always been our home." One doll floated in front of the rest. "This will always be my home. And when you join me, you will be here forever, too."

The doll raised its hand, pointing at my heart, and a terrible realization gripped me—the spirit didn't just want to scare me.

It wanted me dead.

It wanted me to join it in the afterlife.

Trapped in this house.

Forever.

"No," I whispered. "No. I'm going to get out of here. I'm going to save Tara."

"When you wouldn't save your sister?" the doll asked. "When you wouldn't save me?"

"You're not Isabella," I replied. "She would never do this to me. She would never threaten to hurt me or Tara."

An earsplitting cackle filled the room, the dolls shaking with laughter and the books rustling their pages.

"Perhaps. Perhaps not. What does it matter? In the end, you'll still be dead!"

With a terrible howl, the dolls and books dove toward me, and I knew that I was a goner.

37

The dolls and books and toys swarmed me.

I screamed out and closed my eyes as tiny doll hands tugged at my hair, as books snapped at my fingers, as toys poked and prodded every inch of me. I tried to push them away, but there were too many, and I was defenseless—and besides, what was the point in fighting when they had already won? The spirit was right—I couldn't save anyone. I couldn't even save my own sister.

I screamed so loud I didn't even realize someone else was screaming, too, a loud, angry roar that cut above the incessant giggling of the possessed toys.

Moments later, there was a *thud*, the twang of strings, and something clattered against the bureau.

Another smack,

                     another crash.

Were the toys trying to destroy my room, too?

I kept my eyes safely closed, cowering against the door.

Was it my imagination, or were the attacks growing weaker?

I covered my eyes with my hands and peeked through my fingers.

What I saw made me gasp in shock.

38

Tara stood there, racket in hand, swatting away the toys with a scowl on her face.

She hit a few more of them with her racket, causing one ceramic doll to shatter when it hit the wall.

"You'll never take her," Tara said, smacking a book that tried to snap at her shin. "You'll never take either of us. You. Are. Nothing!"

Instantly, all the toys and books dropped to the ground with a resounding *thud*.

Silence stretched between us, broken only by our ragged breaths.

Tara reached out.

"Come on," she said. She glanced over her shoulder at my closet, the door of which was thrown open. "They tied me up with those fake cobwebs; sorry it took me so long to escape. Are you okay?"

"I'm okay," I said. I didn't take her hand or get off the floor. "But what are we going to do?" Tears welled up in my eyes. Because even though she'd fought off the toys, we still had no way of defeating the spirit that trapped us here.

"I had a lot of time to think while I was in there," Tara said. "And I think I have an idea. You invited the spirit in, right?"

"Right. But I tried to uninvite it, I swear. It didn't work. Nothing works."

She shook her head. "You can't just take back an invitation to a spirit like that. That's not how it works. The spirit came in for a reason."

"Yeah, to torment me."

"Maybe. But why this spirit in particular?"

I shrugged.

"Because you wanted your *sister*."

"And it's not my sister."

Tara knelt down in front of me and put a hand on my knee.

"You miss Isabella. And that creates a hole in your heart. There's only one way to fix that."

"I know," I said grumpily, because nothing she said seemed like it would fix this, or get us any closer to ending the nightmare. "Move on. I've tried."

"I know you have," she said. "And you will. But maybe we have to try something else, too. Something more immediate."

"Like what?"

She bit her lip and squeezed my knee.

"Like reaching out to your *real* sister. Reaching out to her was the reason all of this started. Maybe finding her is the way to finish it."

"But how? The spirit board is at your house." *The one I made is just dust!*

"I don't think we need it. All this spiritual activity has probably made the veil between the worlds thin. Come on. I have an idea."

She stood and held out her hand again.

I had no idea what she was planning on doing,

but I knew from the look in her eyes that I couldn't let her down. Even though I knew that no matter what, I would.

Isabella was right.

I couldn't save anyone.

But I was going to try.

39

When we left my room, it was clear the spirit wasn't going to give up without a fight.

"What in the world . . . ?" Tara whispered.

The hallway stretched far, far into the distance, the end disappearing in shadow. The hall itself twisted and turned, the walls buckling or tilting to the sides like in a fun house. Doors opened and slammed shut along the walls, dozens of them, some emitting red light, others green fog. Thick black tar oozed down the walls, dripping from a ceiling that sagged with the weight of decay, paint and wallpaper chipped and peeling. The tar oozed between and over the photographs, all of which were now calling out from their frames, cursing me and calling me terrible names. And the smell . . . It smelled like garbage stuck outside on a hot summer's day.

I gagged and covered my nose with my sleeve. Tara did the same.

"What are we supposed to do now?" I yelled over the slamming of doors.

"We have to find your sister's room!" she said. She gripped my hand tighter. "Come on."

We took a step forward, our feet sinking into the squishy carpet as if it were made of worms.

I looked down.

The carpet *was* worms! And the moment we moved, the hall twisted and stretched and dozens more doors appeared. My vision swayed, and I leaned against Tara to steady myself. I tried to ignore the feeling of warm worms oozing under my toes, slipping over my socks.

"How are we going to find it?" I asked, pointing to the dozens of doors. "It could be any of them."

"We'll know," Tara said. I glanced over at

her—her face was set in determination. When I glanced back to the hall, I swear I heard her whisper, "I hope."

We squished our way forward.

The first door we passed slammed open, revealing not a room, but a graveyard covered in fog and dusted with an eerie green light.

"Not that one," I muttered. We kept going.

The next door was closed. I reached out to the doorknob as we neared, but before I could touch it, it slammed outward with a burst of hot air. I stumbled back and steadied myself on the wall—tar congealed on my fingers, sticky and black. I quickly peeled my hand away, though it was much more difficult than it should have been.

As if the tar were latching on to me.

Trying to pull me in closer.

40

The door that had opened was definitely not Isabella's room—lava pooled in the middle of a giant crater, like the middle of a volcano. Tara grabbed my hand and quickly pulled me forward.

Every room we passed was another nightmare.

We reached the next door, which slammed open, revealing a silver lake—a silver lake, pristine, save the multiple shark fins slicing the surface. The waters sloshed toward us, over the threshold, threatening to fill the hallway and drown us or bring in the sharks. Tara slammed the door shut, and we trudged on.

I didn't want to open the next door. Tara gripped the knob with shaking hands and opened it. A tunnel stretched from the door, light flickering from candles in the wall, illuminating the open coffins lining the hallway. And the figures shuffling toward us.

"Zombies!" I yelped, and she slammed the door shut just as a near one reached out its gnarled hand, trying to pull us inside. We trudged through the worms, making our way to the next door.

"Should we?" she asked.

"I don't want to," I whispered. But I knew, deep down, we didn't really have a choice. We had to find Isabella's room if we were to have any hope of escaping and ending this.

I reached out and pulled the door open. Inside was a pitch-black room. Then light flickered and revealed a woman with glowing green eyes. She opened her fanged mouth and screamed like a banshee, so loud I thought it would make my ears bleed.

"It's no use!" I yelled over the ringing in my ears.

"Don't give up!" Tara called, though I could tell she was no longer as assured or determined.

She was clearly thinking what I was—not being able to find Isabella's room was one thing, but would we ever be able to find the exit? The hallway seemed to go on and on forever, and the farther we went, the farther away from our destination we seemed to go.

What if this was just leading us to a dead end? Literally?

Chills trickled down the back of my neck. It felt like I was being watched.

I turned slowly.

And there, in the middle of the floor, surrounded by worms and snakes and shadows, was the white rabbit, its eyes glowing red.

The moment it saw me, it scurried off and through the doorway with the shark-filled lake. The door slammed shut behind it. And didn't open again.

"I have an idea," I said. I turned around fully. "Come on."

"But that's the way we came!"

"Trust me," I said, and led her toward the closed door.

41

Every step we took toward the closed door was harder.

Our feet sunk deep into the worms, deeper with every step. They sucked and pulled at our legs, dragging us down. We sunk up to our waists, wading through the worms and trying not to yell out as they slipped and slid around us.

Finally, we made our way to the door. I could just barely reach the handle. When I twisted it and yanked the door open, it wasn't Isabella's room that I saw, but the porch.

The way out!

Tara looked at me. She kept her arms high above

her head so she didn't have to touch the worms.

"Go!" I said. "You first. Come on, we can get out of here."

"But we have to get rid of the spirit."

"No, we have to get out of here. We can deal with it later. Just go, hurry!"

Because the more we stood there, the faster we sunk. The worms were up to my chest. They wriggled and squirmed, and I felt sick to my stomach.

Tara didn't argue. She reached for the doorjamb and grabbed on hard, pulling herself up. I stayed at her side and helped push. Every inch she gained pushed me deeper into the worms. Until she was finally free, and I was up to my chin. She turned back and reached out.

"Come on!" she said. "Take my hand!"

As she stood there, the door started to close. She reached out with her other hand and pressed against it, but it didn't stall. The door pressed against her, moved by an otherworldly force. In seconds, I knew, it would push her away.

"No," I said. "It wants me. Get out. Get help." I

tried to smile. It was difficult with worms squirming past my lower lip. "It's like you said: I have to
face this."

"Maria, no!" She reached into the worms, trying to find my hand. I didn't reach back. The door
pressed against her, harder, pushing her back, so
there was barely a foot of open space.

"Go," I said.

Tara yelled my name.

I closed my eyes.

I'm sorry I couldn't save you, Isabella. I'm sorry.
For everything.

And as the door locked tight between my friend
and me, I let myself sink into the worms.

42

Soft warmth surrounded me, a darkness so deep it was almost comforting.

Light shifted.

Sensation shifted.

And when I was finally brave enough to open my eyes, I realized I wasn't surrounded by worms.

I was surrounded by comforters and blankets. Curled up on the floor.

I jolted upright and pushed the blankets away, trying to take in the scene around me.

I was no longer in the hallway.

I was in our fort. Only now it was huge, the size

of a house, filled with glittering lights and plush pillows. It was completely empty.

Empty, save the rabbit in the center of the floor.

Its eyes weren't glowing red this time. It just sat there, staring up at me blankly, and for the briefest moment, I had the thought that I was waking up from a dream.

Then I saw something flicker from the corner of my eye.

A freestanding mirror in the corner.

And there I saw Isabella.

I gasped. My heart leaped into my throat. Because I knew without doubt that it was her. It was *her*.

She smiled at me when she saw me looking. Her reflection was faint, translucent, but it didn't fade. I scrambled to my feet and walked over to her.

"Isabella," I whispered.

She nodded.

"What's going on?"

"I've heard you calling," she said. I collapsed to my knees at the sound of her voice. It wasn't laced with evil, wasn't an imposter. It was kind and loving and *her*. "But the spirit that you invited in had blocked me out. It fed on your fear and your pain, and that energy put up a wall I couldn't push through. It was only now, when you were willing to sacrifice yourself to save Tara, that I was able to reach you."

I looked around. The room wavered, but not because it was an illusion—tears streamed down my cheeks, and my heart ached. I wanted nothing more than to reach out to Isabella, to take her hand, but I feared that if I did, she would fade.

After all, she was nothing but a reflection in the mirror.

"Is it gone?" I asked.

"No," she said sadly. "But I was able to create a sanctuary where I could speak with you. I can't hold it for much longer. You still need to banish the spirit that came in my place. You still have to face it."

"But how? What do I do?"

"It feeds on your pain," Isabella said simply.

"But I'm not afraid," I said. *Not with you here.* "Not anymore."

"No," she said gently. "Your *pain*. This entire time you've wanted forgiveness from me. But deep inside you're hurting because you can't forgive yourself." She knelt down beside my reflection, and I could smell her shampoo, could almost feel the warmth of her. "You have to face it. Not the future. Not being alone. You have to face the past and forgive yourself. Only then will there be nothing for the ghost to feed on. Only then will we be able to banish it, once and for all."

Just her words were enough to bring up the memory. The cold and the dark and the blaring headlights, the screech of the horn. I shoved it away, as I had done ever since that terrible night.

"But I'm scared," I whispered. "It hurts too much."

"I'll be right here. By your side. Just as I always was, and always will be. There was never any reason to seek my forgiveness—I never held anything against you."

The room shifted. This time, it *wasn't* from my tears. The walls of the fort billowed and threatened to collapse. Lights flickered and darkened. I knew it was the evil spirit trying to break in.

"Come," she said. She pointed to the rabbit. "It's time we ended this. Together."

I swallowed my fear and picked up the rabbit. Stared into its black eyes.

I felt myself falling. Falling into the blackness.

Falling into the memory.

The room vanished.

And the night I'd tried so hard to forget came screaming back into focus.

43

Streetlamps cast a faint light on the street, and the night lay heavy over the neighborhood.

Isabella and I played in the front yard. It was getting hard to see, so we were just tossing a ball back and forth, talking idly about the show we had just watched and what our superpowers would be.

"I'd want to fly," she said. "Or walk through walls. Like a ghost!"

"You'd make a good ghost," I said, tossing the ball to her. "You're already so creepy."

She stuck out her tongue at me and bounced the ball back.

"What would yours be? The power to turn into a slug? Oh, wait, you already are one."

I laughed and bounced the ball toward her, harder than I meant to. It flew past her and out into the street.

"I'll get it," she said.

Mom had told us not to go into the road.

It was dark.

The street was empty.

At least, I thought it was.

I was kneeling down to tie my shoe when I heard it. Saw it.

The screech of tires. The flash of lights.

As the car swerved around the corner, far too fast.

As it hit my sister.

I screamed.

Too late. Too late.

I pushed myself to standing, about to run over, when a hand clamped gently on my shoulder. I looked over to see Isabella standing there, looking safe and whole, if a little translucent.

"You see?" she asked. "It wasn't your fault."

"But the ball. I didn't mean to throw it so hard."

"I know."

"And if I had been paying attention, I might have seen the car—"

"You wouldn't have."

She put both of her hands on my shoulders, made me face her and look into her big brown eyes.

"You have to forgive yourself. You didn't know this would happen. You have to let go of the pain. Otherwise, none of us will ever be able to move on."

I swallowed hard. I looked to the street. But there was no more street.

We were back in the fort, and walls shuddered as the spirit outside fought to get in.

"Forgive yourself," she said. "Let go."

I nodded. Looked down to my feet. And let the tears fall.

I'd hated myself for the last few months because of what had happened.

I'd told myself it was all my fault.

I could have saved her.

I could have saved her.

Isabella pulled me in, hugging me tightly even though she felt as faint as smoke.

"I love you," she whispered.

"I love you, too," I said.

And then I closed my eyes and told myself the words I never thought I could.

It wasn't your fault. You didn't mean for it to happen. You have to let it go.

I felt a warmth fill my chest. Not happiness, no. Sadness, for sure. But acceptance, too. It wasn't everything, but it was a start.

"Thank you," I whispered to Isabella.

"Thank you for being my sister," she replied. She stepped back and took my hand. "But this isn't over. Not yet."

The fort door burst open, and in rushed the spirit that had been haunting me.

44

Now that it was no longer pretending to be my sister, I could see the spirit for what she truly was.

And she was horrible.

She was not a young girl, but an old woman, with tangled gray hair and wrinkled skin and hollow black eyes. She snarled when she swept in, her teeth filed to points, and raised her clawed hands like a tiger ready to pounce.

Isabella was faster. She swept in front of me and held out her hand.

The terrible spirit stopped, as if smashing against an invisible shield.

"She forgave herself," Isabella said smugly. "Which means your evil can no longer keep me away."

"You are just little girls," the specter menaced. "You have no chance against the likes of me!"

"We may just be little girls," Isabella said. "But we are more powerful than you'll ever know."

She looked over her shoulder at me. I walked up to her side and held out my own hand toward the specter. Like we were playing make-believe once more. Except this time, I wasn't imagining the current of electricity that buzzed from my heart to my fingertips.

"I have my sister," I said to the evil spirit. "Which means you're not welcome here anymore. Now, get. Out!"

Together, Isabella and I thrust our hands forward. Warm golden light spilled from our palms, pushing the spirit backward. The spirit screamed, but not in anger—in defeat.

"You'll never get rid of me!" she howled. "I will find my way back!"

"No," Isabella said. "You won't. I won't let you."

Isabella looked at me.

"I have to go now. But I'll be with you. Always. I promise."

My heart ached, though I still smiled.

"I know. I love you."

"I love you, too," she said.

Then she turned and faced the evil spirit.

Without flinching, she ran forward and leaped at the old woman, wrapping her arms around the spirit.

The two of them stumbled backward. Out the fort door.

And then they were gone.

45

"One more time," Lauren said. *"Please?"*

Almost a week had passed since Isabella and I had banished the evil spirit. A week of class and homework and no new spiritual sightings—either of the evil spirit or of Isabella.

Around us, the walls of the blanket fort twinkled with lights, and upstairs, my mom and dad sang together as they cooked a big Friday-night feast together. I could already smell the delicious scents and couldn't wait.

But I supposed there was time for one more retelling.

"Okay, okay," I said. "But let me go change into pajamas first."

"Fiiiine," Lauren said, and she flopped back on the pillows.

"It really happened," Tara said, nudging Lauren with her toe.

"I still don't believe it," Lauren said.

Truth be told, she'd had me tell the story of Tara's visit and the haunting a dozen times. Tara had also shared her side of the story, about being trapped in my bedroom closet and wrapped in Halloween decorations, and then how we'd fought our way through the hallway only so she could end up locked outside the house with no way to get back in.

Until, moments later, I had opened it and stepped out.

As if no time had passed since she'd left the hallway.

As if nothing had happened.

Even though, as I'd told them both a dozen times, *everything* had happened.

I made my way to the kitchen. Dad was singing

while he cooked, and he took my hand and spun me around, laughing, before letting me go and turning back to his meal. Mom cast me a happy look. I don't know if it was the banishing of the evil spirit that had made them both happier, or maybe something else had happened on their drive. All I knew was, things seemed to be back to normal.

We were laughing again.

Eating meals together again.

Like a family.

And even though Isabella was gone, I knew she was still there. I felt her in my heart.

Upstairs, I passed by my parents' room and then paused outside Isabella's. We kept the door open now. Everything was as she'd left it. It no longer felt like a cold tomb. It no longer felt like we were hiding from the past.

Even though looking in made my heart hurt, just a little.

Just because we were moving forward didn't mean the past didn't hurt sometimes. I was learning that was okay. I was learning that was not only how we moved forward but how we honored those we lost—both by feeling the ache, and by letting the joyous moments of life filter in.

I went into my room and changed into my pj's, grabbing my stuffed rabbit from the bed as I left.

Clutching it to my chest, I walked down the hall. It was time to move forward.

It was time to live.

Epilogue

I stood by the window in Tara's room. She was at my side.

Outside, the spirit board stuck out of the trash bin that had been pulled to the edge of the street.

We were watching, waiting for it to be picked up. The garbage truck turned the corner, heading our way.

"It's over," Tara said.

I reached over and hugged her, watching as the truck neared.

Only . . .

Right before it reached the bin, a group of kids

on bikes passed by. One of them stopped. Looked at the spirit board.

And before I could say or do anything, he grabbed it from the bin and shoved it into his backpack.

"No!" I yelled, and smacked my hand against the window.

But it was too late. He and his friends took off down the street. I swore I heard the spirit of the old woman cackle victoriously as the kids rode off with the board—and the vengeful ghost attached to it.

I looked at Tara. Her eyes were wide.

"It's going to happen again," I whispered. And there was nothing we could do to stop it.

About the Author

K. R. Alexander is the pseudonym for author Alex R. Kahler.

As K. R., he writes creepy middle grade books for brave young readers. As Alex—his actual first name—he writes fantasy novels for adults and teens. In both cases, he loves writing fiction drawn from true life experiences. (But this book can't be real . . . can it?)

Alex has traveled the world collecting strange and fascinating tales, from the misty moors of Scotland to the humid jungles of Hawaii. He is always on the move, as he believes there is much more to life than what meets the eye.

You can learn more about his travels and books, including *The Collector, The Fear Zone,* and the books in the Scare Me series, on his website cursedlibrary.com.

He looks forward to scaring you again . . . soon.